She walked closer to him. "I enjoyed the carriage ride and lunch. Oh." She waved her hand at the house and yard. "And your letting me talk about changes in the house seems to establish that more firmly in my mind. I'm even more inclined to have the changes made. It's a big house, and should be shared."

He nodded. "I'll put together plans and costs. I understand you might want another company's opinion. That's how business is done." He wasn't sure he should speak the thought that occurred to him, but it came out anyway. "Business has its place. Friendship is separate."

Her gaze shifted away from him and he thought he might be assuming too much. He dared venture further. "I thought you saw *me* today instead of Michael."

Her face clouded. "I know you're different. But still, you're such a reminder of him." She reached up and he thought she was about to touch his hair, maybe brush it off the side of his forehead. He felt it there, felt the light breeze teasing his face. The way her fingertips might feel if she did that.

She shook her head, and her hand fell and found a place in the pocket of her shorts.

He decided to try to jest. "I'll dye my hair if that helps."

At her small laugh he had to smile. "Shave my head?"

"Would you really go that far?"

"No." All teasing aside, he said, "If you can't see me as anyone other than a reminder of Michael, a change of my hair wouldn't do it." He paused. "Would it?"

"No." She looked serious, too.

Books by Yvonne Lehman

Love Inspired Heartsong Presents

The Caretaker's Son
Lessons in Love

YVONNE LEHMAN

Yvonne Lehman is an award-winning bestselling author of fifty books, including mystery, romance, young adult, women's fiction and mainstream historical. She founded the Blue Ridge Mountains Christian Writers Conference and directed it for twenty-five years, and she now directs the Blue Ridge "Autumn in the Mountains" Novel Retreat, held annually at the Ridgecrest/LifeWay Conference Center near Asheville, North Carolina.

YVONNE LEHMAN

Lessons in Love

HEARTSONG
PRESENTS

Recycling programs
for this product may
not exist in your area.

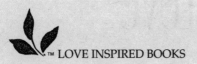

™ LOVE INSPIRED BOOKS

ISBN-13: 978-0-373-48670-0

LESSONS IN LOVE

www.LoveInspiredBooks.com

Printed in U.S.A.

Such things were written in the Scriptures long ago to teach us. They give us hope and encouragement as we wait patiently for God's promises.

—*Romans* 15:4

My writers group, who give story advice
and suggestions when I'm at the early idea stage,
and who helped choose the name of my hero, Noah.

Ray Blackston for his mission trip information.

A special thanks to Cindy,
who accompanied me to my setting of
Savannah, Georgia, for fun and research.

Chapter 1

Megan Conley didn't know if it was the heavy rainfall or a trick of her mind that made her think there was a blurry figure on that front porch as she drove past the house of her missing boyfriend, Michael.

A few days ago a dim light had glowed from a front window. By the time she found enough nerve to return, she encountered only a dark, locked house with no car parked either on the street or in back. A couple days ago she'd thought she glimpsed him in his car near the historic tour company. She'd blinked in surprise, and when she looked again, he wasn't there and the car wasn't Michael's.

Neither her mind nor her eyes seemed to work right anymore. Not since she'd received the text message she kept staring at as if it would change. He spelled out the words, instead of using shorthand text, as if that might make things clearer. It didn't.

I'M SORRY. FORGIVE ME.
WILL EXPLAIN LATER.
WITH LOVE, MICHAEL.

She'd signed "with love" on notes to male and female
friends, relatives and even acquaintances and knew it didn't
necessarily mean "I love you." So what was he saying? Where
had he gone—and why?

He'd been gone more than a month. She wasn't able to reach
him by phone. His mom said she didn't know any more than
Megan knew. "Michael is…" Mrs. Nansen had said, paused,
then added, "unpredictable at times. But he's a good boy. He
means well."

Boy?

Michael was 27. Three years older than she. He wasn't exactly a boy. She could think of many excuses for why he might
leave. If he had found someone else, he only had to say so.
In the past months, she'd had a few "say so" thoughts of her
own about Michael.

She was well aware that people changed their minds—and
their hearts. For more than three years, her friend Annabelle
had planned to marry Wesley. But from the moment Symon
DeBerry Sinclair returned to Savannah, he and Annabelle
began to fall in love. Maybe Michael had fallen in love with
someone else.

Megan pulled into the mall parking lot and found a space
far down the row. After all the media coverage given to Sy
DeBerry, the *New York Times* best-selling author now known
as "Savannah's native son," all the city had probably turned
out for the signing of his latest book.

The rain had stopped, and the afternoon sun shone brightly.
Were it not for the visible humidity rising from the puddles
on the pavement, she'd think it hadn't rained at all but that her
eyes had simply grown hazy rather than filled with the tears
that sometimes threatened lately.

She hurried inside and, upon reaching the bookstore, saw Lizzie and Annabelle near the entrance.

"I should buy a copy of Symon's book," Megan said.

Annabelle gestured to the crowded store. "Look at that line. All of Savannah has come out."

Megan glanced around. "Just what I was thinking."

"Anyway," Lizzie put in. "Annabelle said Symon will give us autographed copies if we'll be nice little bridesmaids and not make a fiasco of their wedding." She shook her head. "I made no promises."

Her mind still elsewhere, Megan took a deep breath as her gaze scanned the corridor. Lizzie took hold of her arm. "Not a good day?"

Annabelle spoke sympathetically. "We can look at dresses another time."

Megan shook her head. "No. I've told you before—don't tiptoe around me. This thing about Michael is more confusing than anything." She sighed. "But…I thought I saw him again."

"Isn't that a possibility?" Lizzie said.

Megan lifted her hands in a helpless gesture. She had no idea where Michael might be.

"Let's get something to drink," Annabelle suggested. "And you can tell us about it."

"We'll look at the dresses first," Megan countered. "Life doesn't stop for me." She meant it and joined in the conversation as they headed for the Bridal Shoppe. They examined several different styles of bridesmaid's dresses. "The strapless might be better for outside."

Lizzie wrinkled her nose. "My shoulders would end up with more freckles."

"Your freckles are beautiful," Annabelle said. "Anyway, wedding ceremonies never last long and the reception tables will have umbrellas."

"But on second thought," Lizzie mused. "If I did get more

freckles, I'd just be auburn skinned. Could join the circus. Maybe meet a man who—"

They continued to chat and joke, and they decided to give more thought and discussion to dresses and plans. When they got to the restaurant, Megan slipped into the booth and sat opposite her friends.

After the waitress came and they ordered sodas, Annabelle reached over and gently tapped Megan's hand. "Now, do you want to talk about having seen Michael?"

Megan sighed. "It's probably my imagination. Or," she said, looking at the sympathetic green eyes of her redheaded friend, "like you said, Lizzie—maybe I did see him. He may still be around and just doesn't want to see me."

Their condescending nods made Megan feel worse. She wasn't one to wallow in...what? Self-pity? Being dumped? Or was Michael sick? "Or," she continued, "maybe his dad or someone else was checking on the house." She slapped the booth's tabletop. "I'm going to forget it. We have a wedding to plan. Annabelle, have you decided on your colors?"

The conversation paused as the waitress brought their drinks. After unwrapping her straw and taking a sip through it, Annabelle said, "Whatcha think? Coral?"

Lizzie screeched and grabbed her mop of thick auburn hair. "Not with this hair. What about blue, to match your eyes?"

"Or," Megan mused. "Spring green. You'll have the white carpeted aisle, white wedding chairs, lush green lawn and backdrop of deeper green trees and bushes. Then there are all those blooming flowers Symon planted. The white arbor can be decorated with vines, flowers and yellow ribbon."

Both stared at her with thoughtful expressions and Lizzie began to nod. Annabelle pointed a graceful finger at her. "You have a knack for this, friend. It's sounding perfect. Now, should the ribbon be satin or mesh or—"

Megan was nodding and smiling about her suggestion being accepted. Then she heard no more. Her gaze focused beyond them to the entrance of the restaurant. Her jaw came unhinged and her mouth opened.

"What?" her friends were saying.

"H-he's there," she whispered.

They turned to look. "Who? Where?"

"He left." Megan took several breaths. "He looked straight at me. And then he turned and walked out."

"Michael?" Annabelle asked.

"Yes." She sighed. "No." She began beating the ice in her glass with her straw, then stopped, moved her hands to her lap and held them. Looking over at her friends, she tried to explain. "That wasn't him. But at first glance I thought it was. H-he looked like Michael."

Now her friends stared at her with pity written all over their faces.

Megan stirred her soda. "Well, I didn't get a good look but he resembled Michael. His hair." She pleaded with her eyes for them to believe her. "You know, nobody has hair like his unless it's from a box."

She remembered even having looked at a box for the exact color and the best she had come up with was light blond, almost platinum. But the sun could make it look golden or silver, depending on the time of day. "He was kind of like an older Michael."

"How old?" Lizzie asked.

"Oh, not old. Couple years, maybe."

"Ah, that explains it." Lizzie declared. "You've said time and again you wished Michael was more mature and serious. Okay, Annabelle has mentioned the children who come to her modeling classes have growing spurts. Michael's been gone a few weeks, had a maturity growing spurt and now—"

Annabelle poked her and Lizzie grimaced. "Sorry. Can't seem to help it."

Megan dismissed the comments with a flick of her hand.

That was part of Lizzie's appeal. She spoke her mind and often before thinking. "About now I could use a little humor."

"Humor?" Lizzie wrinkled her freckled nose. "That's my serious side."

Megan sighed. "I'm getting tired of so much serious stuff." She shook her head. "Maybe it was just the man's hair. It's like I keep looking for Michael. Thinking he's going to show up."

Annabelle nodded. "You could use a good dose of Aunt B."

Megan smiled. "Did a world of good for you."

Annabelle agreed, holding out her hand with the engagement ring on her finger.

Lizzie groaned. "Think it would do anything for me?"

Megan and Annabelle said in unison, "Couldn't hurt."

Chapter 2

Noah Fairfax could kick himself. After all his attempts to remain inconspicuous, he'd walked right into the restaurant where she sat. He'd known she was in the mall. He wouldn't make a good private detective, that's for sure.

What he'd done so far was sit in his car he'd parked a couple spaces away from the trolley on which Megan would be conducting the tour. When she looked his way he'd ducked down, feeling like a criminal. Michael wanted him to make sure Megan was getting on with her life. Noah had felt guilty watching her approach the tour group. But he would feel guiltier if he couldn't give Michael a good report.

He didn't know if he would have recognized Megan Conley in the mall had she not been with the other two women he'd seen in a few pictures Michael had shown him on his phone and on their social media pages. The one with dark hair was very pretty. Michael said she was some kind of beauty queen. And he'd never seen a more colorful person than the one with red hair. He didn't know how to describe women very well, but having some design experience, he supposed if he had to portray Megan he'd say…classic. Nothing outstanding, or detracting. Just…right. A perfect balance for the other two women. All three were gorgeous and he didn't think that opinion was based on his having been away from civilization for the past few years.

After he'd spotted her at the bookstore and watched her walk down the corridor with her friends, all three in high heels with their well-turned calves showing, he'd smiled appreciatively. Then he entered the store to buy one of Sy DeBerry's books. Those thrillers had been among his and some buddies' favorite reading during their few snatches of spare time serving in Iraq. They'd discussed how a book could make sense of senseless killing, while some of their real experiences seemed far from making any sense.

Lately, he'd seen a lot of media coverage about the famous author and thought he'd like to meet him. He stood in line for more than an hour. He didn't want to take up anyone else's time, so he didn't engage in much conversation while getting the autograph. However, the author took time to ask about Noah's connection to Savannah and asked for his business card. After that, Noah thought it was time for a cup of coffee. Maybe he'd start reading the book.

However, the moment he entered the restaurant, he spied the three women in a nearby booth. The brunette and redhead had their backs to him, but while he was staring, Megan looked him right in the face and registered surprise. He knew she noticed his resemblance to Michael. He quickly turned and left, feeling as if he'd done something immoral or illegal.

When he'd first looked, the three women seemed happy, in casual conversation, and Megan's face was soft with pleasure. He hoped she wasn't devastated by Michael's actions.

Michael and the military had increased Noah's prayer life. Now he wondered what in the world would have happened with Michael had he not prayed for him. Michael was foolish for not confiding in Megan Conley and for just leaving like that. But it could have been worse. He shuddered to think it could have turned out like the disaster with Loretta.

However, in spite of that positive aspect, he also knew some reactions to life's situations were immediate, and some were delayed. People could put up a good front. Megan Conley certainly made a good appearance.

Noah did a little grocery shopping, returned home and discovered he didn't have half the things he needed and had a lot of stuff he didn't need. So he made a whopping sandwich and noted even that turned his kitchen into a mess hall, and his culinary attempt was simply chow.

One thing he could make was a hot cup of instant coffee. He settled at the kitchen table with the sandwich of deli meat, mayonnaise, lettuce, tomato and cheese between slices of whole wheat bread. He laid the book aside and chomped through the sandwich rather than let tomato juice drip on the new book.

When he finally got to the novel he was instantly engrossed. When the female character came onto the page, described as having flowing honey-colored hair, Noah's mind reverted to Megan Conley. Hers was like that. Flowing. Down around her shoulders. Maybe…dark honey, with those golden-brownish—

He shut the book and tried to divert his mind from going off on a tangent where it didn't belong.

Sure, he could keep Michael's confidence because he thought Michael would go off the deep end if he didn't. Noah had seen many guys do that. But he couldn't do this snooping like Michael asked him to do. He didn't need to hide from Miss Conley. He was not a sneak and didn't intend to live like one. And for now, he'd take a historic tour to…wherever Miss Conley might lead.

He called to make sure it wasn't her night off. He learned she would be leading the hop-on/hop-off trolley tour that evening, which would suit his purpose of being obvious and accessible.

Because this wasn't the time or place to wear a helmet or a hard hat, he found a baseball cap Michael had left on a shelf in a bedroom closet. It covered most of his hair, the distinguishing feature about him and Michael that used to initiate glances and conversation. That hadn't been an issue during the past years when his was cut in a conservative military style.

He wore the cap at the trolley stop, although he felt it was contrary to his personality. When he stopped near her as each one in the group stepped up into the trolley, he knew he was not disguised. Her reaction was like it had been in the restaurant—surprised. Her lips parted slightly, and she inhaled audibly. Then her brown eyes, darker than honey, maybe like dark chocolate, first held a question and then something akin to a warning.

He felt like saying, "No, I am not Michael." He didn't have that so-called boyish charm. He was much more reserved than Michael and to prove it, he simply said, "Good evening," handed her his ticket and stepped up into the big red trolley. The hot, humid late-summer afternoon wasn't the only thing making him sweat.

Now he realized this excursion was not the thing to do. But what was? Keep showing up where she might be and hope she thought nothing of it? That was stupid. Go up to her and say that Michael asked him to make sure she was doing all right? That would be worse.

Maybe he should reenlist and return to Iraq. He was out of touch with relationships. Never been too good with them, come to think of it. That was Michael's department.

Here he was, finding a seat near the back of the trolley, feeling like an idiot and having no idea where to go from there. He should go home, but if he rose from his seat and approached her now she'd probably have him arrested for harassment.

After everyone boarded, she stepped inside, leaned over and spoke to the driver. About him, probably. He looked out the window, feeling the summer wind and viewing the lush

green of Spanish moss-laden trees. A few weeks ago the azaleas lining the street had been a brilliant array of color, the
red particularly dazzling. Quite a contrast to the bland Iraqi
sand. However, without staring at her, he was very much aware
of the young woman in black pants and white short-sleeved
shirt bearing the circular historic tour logo. Her dark-honey
hair was slicked back from her face and fastened in a ponytail.

"Welcome to the historic tour," she began, each word distinct and warm. "I'm Megan Conley, and I'll be relaying much
of the history of Savannah, one of our nation's most popular
vacation spots." She briefly established her qualifications for
leading the tour. She'd minored in history at college, led tours
during summer vacation and after graduating last year had become a full-time guide.

She relayed that in the 1950s, a group of women had orga-
nized to save and preserve the city's historic charm and structures. By 1966 the historic district was designated a National
Historic Landmark, one of the largest in the country.

Seeing her glance at him, Noah had the feeling that look
meant he should be aware that this woman wasn't one to be
toyed with. He did his best to appear as stoic as the statues
in the squares, lest she think he had any ulterior motives. Reminding himself he had every right to be there, he smiled at
the pleasant-looking middle-aged man next to him and relaxed when the trolley began to roll. A welcome breeze blew
in through the window as he listened to her tell about General James Edward Oglethorpe, who established the colony of
Georgia in 1733 at the age of thirty-seven.

Thirty-seven.

Eight years older than Noah. A brief thought crossed his
mind as he wondered what he would have accomplished by
the time he reached thirty-seven. His attention was drawn to
Megan again. He felt like a man with a divided mind. A part
of him could not help but wonder how Michael could have
abandoned her.

But he knew why, even if he couldn't imagine how. At the same time he heard the words coming from her intriguing, full, expressive lips. "Oglethorpe laid out the city of Savannah in a perfect pattern of squares," she was saying. "The Trustees adopted the Latin motto *'Non Sibi Sed Aliis.'* It means, 'Not for self, but for others.'" She smiled and added, "Others, like you."

Looking around, Noah knew she endeared the tourists to her with her manner and words. When the trolley stopped for the group to walk along the sidewalk for information and then go inside a historic mansion, Noah decided to hop off the tour.

He'd done what he intended by letting her see him out in the open with nothing to hide. "Thank you," he said, stepping down in front of her. "I have another appointment."

He was faced with the questioning expression of a lovely woman. But this was not the time or place for explanation, so he hastened from the group gathering on the sidewalk waiting to go inside the building.

He knew he needed to summon her to the house, but he had no idea what he'd say when she arrived. To her, he'd likely be a mere unwelcome reminder of the man she'd loved who had mysteriously departed.

Chapter 3

Megan didn't realize how uptight she was until after she watched the jeans-clad, platinum-haired man in the baseball cap stroll along the square, away from the group. Any other time she might consider him just another tourist. He'd looked all right and had been polite. But you couldn't judge a person by that. Many times after someone committed a terrible act, those interviewed said they never would have suspected it.

She never would have suspected Michael would desert her without an explanation. And someone showing up who reminded her strongly of Michael had to be more than coincidence.

But what was it?

Forcing herself to let go of thoughts about the man, she continued the two-hour tour, hoping she didn't sound as mechanical as she felt. After it ended, not wanting to go home and be alone with all her unanswered questions, Megan accepted Carl's invitation to go for ice cream. He was a beloved member of the church she attended and a retired history teacher who loved Savannah. He and Aunt B had taught at the same school. His wife had died a few years ago, so he began leading tours to fill his empty hours. He preferred leading the carriage tours.

Megan could be honest with Carl about her confusion concerning Michael. Carl was sweet and kind. She didn't need to rant and rave to him. She'd vented to Annabelle and Lizzie until she felt rather rusty. She and Carl sat in the little corner restaurant and soothed their concerns with hot-fudge sundaes.

She didn't mention the man who kept appearing; she tried to forget him and just enjoy Carl's company. They talked about the weather with its seasonally hot and humid days, topped off with lovely warm evenings. They exchanged a couple stories about tourist incidents.

But she knew his question would come. And it did, right after he licked the fudge from his spoon, turned it over and licked the inside. His kind blue eyes stared into hers and he spoke softly. "You doing all right?"

She was ready for that. Annabelle's Aunt B had encouraged her to do something different that appealed to her instead of focusing on Michael. The tours helped, but many times Michael had been with her on them and now she was always aware of his absence.

After licking her spoon, she took a sip of water lest she talk with a smudge of chocolate on her lip, like Carl had. With a tilted chin she informed him, "I have a new interest."

"See?" He leaned his gray head toward her. "I told you—"

She shook her head. "No. Not a man." Her lifted hand warded off that notion. "No more men for me."

The laugh lines appeared around his eyes as he smiled. "The right one will come along."

A man simply was not on her agenda. But someone like Carl would be a consideration if one was. That is, if he were about thirty years younger and just as wise and mature as Carl.

"Watercolors," she said.

His brows shot up and he gave a nod. "So you're an artist."

She took another spoonful of ice cream and let it cool her throat as it slid down. "I've dabbled in it and have taken a few art courses. Annabelle is writing a children's book about a cat's bad hair day. It's based on Aunt B's cat, SweetiePie, a beautiful white Persian." Megan laughed. "It's really hilarious."

"I'd love to see it."

"Okay." She grabbed a paper napkin and, although she usually sketched with a pencil, took a pen from her purse and quickly sketched the cat's face with pen marks indicating the hair in disarray. She pushed it over to him. "That's how the cat looks after being in a muddy creek."

Carl's hearty laugh delighted her. "That's great. Kids will love it."

An element of doubt laced her words. "Annabelle's fiancé, Symon, says the editor has to love it first."

"I'll bet he will." He almost convinced her.

Her head turned toward the window. The sky had darkened. "I might work on that for a while tonight."

Not liking the idea that her hastily sketched cat would be wadded up and tossed into the trash—or become a clean-up device for spills and splatters—she folded the napkin and tucked it into her tote bag. She would dispose of it properly or determine if she could use that flow of artistic impulse. Sometimes the best results came with little effort instead of by struggling to get a sketch just right.

Carl insisted the sundaes were his treat. After walking the couple blocks to their cars, parked near each other on the street where the tours ended, she thanked him, jumped into her car and locked the doors. She did that automatically most of the time, but tonight she was acutely aware of the unknown. She watched as Carl ambled down to his car. A few people were strolling along the sidewalks. She saw no lone person.

Out on the street, she looked into the rearview mirror more than she looked ahead, wondering if the fair-haired man might follow her. No one seemed to be. But he was the same man she saw at the restaurant. And if he was the man on Michael's porch when the rain fell so heavily, he likely knew where she lived. Lizzie wouldn't be home from her work at the Pirate's Cave until after ten. That meant Megan would be alone at the house for about an hour.

She'd be careful.

After she left the main road, she was more aware than usual of the dark houses and deserted streets. The moon kept hiding behind scattered clouds. While on the trolley, she'd watched carefully for any inadvertent move by the man. He hadn't given her any reason to fear him. Not even a sly look or an ogle. Had he not reminded her of a Michael imposter...

She almost laughed at that half thought, despite the ominous things going on around her. But reason, as much as she could make of this unreasonable situation, told her he had been at Michael's house. He did know who she was or he wouldn't have left the restaurant when he saw her. Then he showed up at the tour so she would see him. Was he up to no good and becoming braver? Had he harmed Michael?

Like the shock of a giant flashlight being thrust into the darkness, the lights around Michael's house blazed like a neon sign flashing "come into my lair, said the spider to the fly." A car parked on the street in front of the house seemed a sure signal he wanted her to come there.

Instinct told her to call someone. Maybe Symon. But his publisher had come to town. He and Annabelle would be at Aunt B's. She might call Lizzie's brother, Paul. Or even have the police come. But what would she say? That a man who resembled Michael had joined her tour and now the lights were on at Michael's house?

He hadn't threatened her in any way. The police would probably arrest *her* for being a threat to society. Her friends would at least suggest she see a counselor of some kind. Maybe she had fabricated him like children do with imaginary friends.

If this fellow meant any harm, she might as well go ahead

and face it. She had to know what was going on. She turned
into the drive, drove around the house and pulled into the back.
Looking up, she saw the porch light was on and lights glared
from the kitchen windows. Of course, that could change with
the flick of a switch.

In case she needed a quick getaway, she made a sweeping
curve, pointed the front of the car toward the driveway and
parked with the side of the car in front of the garage.

She exited the car, shut the door and pushed the remote.
She emitted a light snort as she remembered the remote button could cause an alarm loud enough to awaken the dead. But
she'd heard alarms before and done nothing, and most people
seemed to tolerate the sound until someone turned off their
offending signal. Everyone would probably ignore it.

She ascended the steps, crossed the deck and rang the doorbell. Then she backed away to the banister.

He opened the door immediately, and they stood on opposite sides of the screen. He'd removed the ball cap and for
a moment she could only study him. He stood unmoving, as
if wanting her to know he was no threat. His beautiful hair
looked like someone had mussed it, as she'd often done to Michael's. His face was more serious than Michael's, a smooth,
deeper bronze, and his eyes didn't dance. They looked like he
might have bad news.

But she had to remember his strange actions. If he had
something to tell her, he could have contacted her and made
an appointment. So she kept her finger on the alarm button
and asked, "Are you stalking me?"

He replied, as seriously as he looked, "You're the one standing on my doorstep."

"*Your*...doorstep?" she said.

She stepped back farther as if to escape those words. This
was Michael's house. But...had she assumed too much? She
called her own house on Jones Street her home, but it had really been her grandmother's until she died and left it to Megan.

Only six weeks ago. That hurt so much. She needed to grieve for her grandmother. She had needed Michael to help her grieve. But now she had to keep her thoughts on this moment.

He opened the screen door. She shifted her weight to her right foot, ready to run. He didn't step out, however—he just stood there without the screen as a barrier. "It's late. Would you like to return in the morning and we can talk?" He grimaced slightly. "Midmorning would be best."

He sounded tired—and kind. For an instant she forgot to be afraid. "Are you…his brother or something?" Michael had said he was an only child.

"Cousin," he said, although she hadn't said Michael's name. Maybe he was being kind, knew that sometimes it was difficult saying the name of a person who hurt you or trampled your emotions. Another thought occurred to her. "He never mentioned a cousin."

She wondered if his downcast eyes meant she had caught him in a lie. Then he looked directly at her again. "Do you know of Fairfax-Nansen Construction and Renovations?"

She gave a single nod. Michael's last name was Nansen. He'd said his mother was part owner of the company.

"I'm the Fairfax side of that. Or his son, anyway. I'm Noah Fairfax."

Maybe, she thought. Michael had never mentioned him. If he were a cousin impersonator, he would certainly know of that company. She took a deep breath and realized the air had turned quite cool. A moth flew around the porch light. She switched her attention back to him. "Do you know…" she shrugged, wondering which question to ask. "Is he okay? Where is he? Why?"

"I really can't tell you." His voice sounded sincere. He looked concerned. "Those are questions for Michael to answer."

Well, this was useless. She reverted to her suspicions, not

even knowing what all they were. Her adrenaline began to act up. He said Michael should be the one to answer. But where was Michael? "What should I do? Call out like I'm calling a dog?"

"Not a bad idea," he said as if serious. He opened the screen further and stepped outside, holding on to its frame. She walked sideways to the steps, ready to go. What was with this guy? Was Michael inside?

She intended to push the alarm and run if he made a move. But he stood still.

"Sorry," he said. "I made a bad joke, responding to your calling out. Or maybe not. Call out to God. Pray."

Where did that come from? Was he a weirdo or what? She tried to form the words, but they got stuck behind her puckered mouth. Then it opened and she squeaked. "P-pray?"

He nodded. "Yeah. You know." He turned enough for his shoulder to prop open the screen open and folded his hands together in a prayer position in front of his chest. He ducked his head and closed his eyes for an instant.

Just as quickly, she turned and descended the steps, saying, "I will definitely be praying tonight."

"I will pray for you," he said. "See you in the morning."

On the sidewalk she turned and saw that he stood at the banister, gazing down at her. She hastened to the car, pushed the unlock button and reached for the handle. "If you're going to be as secretive as Michael, what would we have to talk about?"

Her hand halted when he called down his reply. "My… doorstep."

Chapter 4

Megan waited for the single-cup brewer to finish gurgling so she could have her morning wake-up coffee.

After it finished and she took a sip, she sat at the island and told Lizzie about Noah joining the tour and her going to the house. "Maybe I'm crazy."

Lizzie got up and poured water into the machine. "Well, frankly, I'd opt for crazy if I could meet a man similar to Michael." She put the pod in and punched the blue button, which turned to orange. "Or, just a man who's halfway decent."

"But it's so weird." Megan's thoughts were as gurgled as the coffee machine. "Michael vanished. Now this guy appears like a revised version."

Lizzie brought her coffee over and sat across from Megan. "Ohhhh. You mean healthy, wealthy and wise?"

Megan had to laugh. "I think that comes from early to bed and early to rise. Something I'm not too knowledgeable about."

Lizzie moaned. "I don't know why all the intriguing men come to you and Annabelle. Every time I meet a new man and he's a dud I question why, why, why."

Megan sighed. "I don't need this. I wonder what happened to Michael. Now I have to wonder if this cousin is real, a great pretender or if my mind is playing tricks."

"Trick or treat," Lizzie mused. "Oh." Her green eyes widened. "Let me go with you and see if he's real."

But Megan felt she needed to do this alone. She wanted to discover if he was either hiding information about Michael or…hiding Michael.

She showered, dried her hair, fastened it into a ponytail and applied minimal makeup. She wasn't trying to impress— just get some answers—so she dressed in jeans and a T-shirt.

At 10:00 a.m., although doubting he worked there, she called Fairfax-Nansen Construction and Renovations and asked for Noah Fairfax. The voice said, "Just a moment, please. I'll put you through to his cell phone."

After a promotional ad, she heard someone say, "Noah Fairfax."

She wasn't prepared to hear his voice. "I wasn't sure how to reach you."

"I'm waiting for you."

"I'm on my way."

She hadn't said her name. Did he recognize her voice? She almost laughed at that. He had heard it on the tour and at his house last night.

She would insist on staying outside. She was not about to go inside for whatever he was doing in the house she thought belonged to Michael. A few blocks later, she parked the car like she had last night and realized she'd been here only about nine hours ago. She walked up onto the deck and halted, shocked.

A silver-domed serving dish stood on three lion-paw feet in the center of the round table. Two plates and silverware on cloth napkins were positioned opposite each other.

More appealing was the coffeepot. It sat on a small table adjacent to the wall. Considering her few hours of sleep and only one cup this morning, she could use another. However, she didn't know if someone lived here with Noah Fairfax. One of those two cups beside the sugar and creamer set might not be for her. Nor the place setting on the table.

She stood at the banister and looked out at the pristine back-yard, a private haven with its myriad trees and bushes, and the wrought iron fencing that separated it from neighbors. She'd loved walking along the brick paths with Michael.

Hearing the screen door squeak, she turned. Noah came out smiling and holding a glass of orange juice in each hand. He nodded at the table. "Have a seat."

If she still read romance novels instead of those thrillers Symon wrote, she might have been tempted by his smile instead of remembering her suspicions of him, even if she couldn't identify the suspicions. She refused to return the smile that accented his full wide lips that spread over straight white teeth. The smile caused interesting lines at the sides of his eyes.

But of course she'd be comparing his appearance with Michael's. The thought occurred to her that Michael was an intriguing first sketch, whereas this man seemed more like a finished product. But she refused to let her conclusion linger. Instead she glanced at the table. "What is this?"

"Breakfast." He gestured to the place settings.

She could pretend he was a cousin of Michael's and everything was as innocent and appealing as it looked. So she sat. "How do you know I haven't had breakfast?"

"I don't. But I haven't had breakfast," he said, reminding her of Michael in his playful days. He sat and looked at her with his deep blue eyes. "But Michael said his working evenings had meant sleeping in and having brunch. I thought it might be the same for you."

It was, but before she could say more he asked, "Shall we pray?"

She bowed her head but kept her eyes on him. The slant of the morning sun was just beginning to touch his hair with a hint of silver. The prayer sounded sincere and brief, thanking

God for the food and asking that she and Michael give their burdens to the Lord and let Him work them for their good and His glory.

At the amen, he lifted the silver dome. Instantly permeating the fragrant cool morning air was the enticing aroma of scrambled eggs mixed with cheese, strips of crisp bacon, small squares of diced ham and lightly browned biscuits.

Her mouth actually watered. This was much different from what she might get from the freezer and toss into a toaster or pour from a box. She picked up a hot biscuit and, while buttering it, wondered if that's what he was trying to do to her— butter her up. If so, why? "Did you make these from scratch?"

"My cook did." The little lines again fanned out from his eyes. "Her name is supermarket."

"They smell like Willamina's." Seeing his lifted eyebrows, she explained. "She cooks for Aunt B. I call her Aunt B, but she's really the aunt of my friend Annabelle."

"Would that be Miss Brandley, Savannah's most beloved schoolteacher?"

Megan nodded as she filled her plate. "I guess she taught you?"

"Challenged us to learn," he said affectionately, then grinned as he grabbed a piece of bacon. "Too bad nobody taught me to cook. To be honest, the bacon is precooked and the ham came in those little packets already diced."

In case the food was poisoned, she waited until he took a couple bites, then she did, too. "Still good," she said while chewing. Then she swallowed. "And speaking of being honest, what can you tell me about Michael?"

He chewed, swallowed and took a sip of juice. "We talked. He said he had to leave for a while and asked me to make sure you're all right. That's why I've—" He paused and grimaced. "Why I…checked on you."

She laid her fork on her plate, feeling her defenses rise. "How much checking did you do?"

His skin deepened in color as he admitted, "I watched you go to work. I mean, if a person goes to work it's a sign he or she is handling things all right. I didn't mean to be at the restaurant in the mall when you were there. I felt guilty when I saw you, and that's why I turned and left." He sounded contrite and his eyes seemed to plead with her. "That's why I took the tour—so you could see that I meant no harm and you could talk to me if you wished."

She lifted her chin. "What if I hadn't come here last night?"

He took a deep breath and exhaled. "I would have gone about my business and told Michael I'm not a private detective or an intermediary."

"You know where he is?"

He shook his head. "He said he'd let me know."

At least it sounded like Michael hadn't been harmed. Or wasn't ill somewhere. And she was hungry, so she picked up her fork and stabbed a square of ham. When that was down, she asked, "Do you know what his problem is?"

"To a great extent." He paused, looking down, poking at his food. "But I only returned from Iraq six months ago. We were at odds when I enlisted several years ago." He seemed to choose his words carefully, thoughtfully, then met her gaze again. "In the past weeks we've tried to get back to the way we were years ago. Very close."

"Have you?"

"No. It's a process."

"What was the problem?"

"He can't trust me if I betray his confidence. This is a crisis period for him. I want to help, not hinder."

She thought about that. "So," she said slowly, after her mouth was clear again. "Is his problem with you or with me?"

"With himself." He leaned forward. "It affects you and me, obviously. But it's not a problem with you." His voice softened. "He thinks you're the most wonderful woman in the world."

Trying to cover the irritation welling up inside, Megan reached for the silver dome. He beat her to it and lifted the lid. "That's just ducky." She took a biscuit, opened a tight-lidded jar, picked up her knife and began to slather apple butter on the biscuit. "He walks out on the most wonderful woman in the world…" She didn't try to keep the sarcasm from her voice. "And leaves her high and dry without an explanation." She scoffed at that and at too much apple butter. "Imagine what he might have done with someone…less wonderful."

She slapped the two sides of the biscuit together and took a big bite. Chewing, she tried to think of how to redeem herself. Just like the sudden sweep of grief when she'd think of her grandmother, she sometimes felt the sweep of Michael's abandonment and didn't know how to describe it. Hurt. Disappointment. Confusion. But it inevitably manifested itself in anger.

"I'm sorry," she apologized. "I shouldn't take it out on you. Seems we're both, like you said, affected."

He began to slather apple butter on a biscuit. "You'll be all right," he said, as if he were some kind of counselor she should listen to. "Just bear with Michael and let him work through this crisis period and pray for him. Have faith that he will be that great guy he used to be."

She wasn't sure what "great guy" that was. They'd only been in the process of getting to know each other. Or that's what she'd thought. She picked up her glass of orange juice.

"Michael said you're a fine Christian woman."

She put her glass down and stared across at him. "What did he mean? That he can be as secretive and missing as he wants and I'll sit around waiting until he—" Her gaze lifted to the porch ceiling for a moment. "Until he finds himself?" Sarcasm again.

He sighed. "I don't know. I didn't ask to be in the middle of this. But my role is to help Michael in any way. And you, if I can."

"You're going to cook for me?"

He grimaced. "This is the best I can do, and don't even ask

what happened to the first batch of eggs." He sounded so pitiful she almost laughed. Then he leaned forward, his blue eyes
gazing into hers. "But I could learn."

Just as she thought he might be flirting, he leaned back
again and blew out air between pursed lips. "Sorry. I don't
mean to give the wrong impression of my intentions. I don't
have any. I mean—"

"Don't worry," she snapped. "I wouldn't be receptive, anyway."

"Good." He leaned back. "That's settled."

"Now," she said. "You invited me here to talk about your
doorstep."

"I did," he said as if surprised, "didn't I?"

She nodded.

"Hmmm. I was just making what I thought was a clever
quip. My intentions were really to atone for giving the impression I'm a sneak or a stalker."

"This is rather blatant." She waved at the table.

"Did it work? I mean…" He grinned. "Do you forgive me?"

"Are you sorry?"

He hesitated before answering. "No. I really want to know
if you're all right."

"What is all right? Waiting for Michael? Forgetting him?"

He said sincerely, "I don't know."

Neither did she. "What do you think Michael would do if
you told him I wasn't all right?"

He opened his mouth as if to speak, then stood. "Let me
move the table out of the sun."

His head bent over the table as he grasped the edges, his
hair, touched by the slanting silver rays of the morning sun,
presenting an aura.

She remembered the last time she'd seen Michael. He'd
said, "We need to talk."

Their talk had been mainly about his not feeling well. Seeing the doctor. Being on an antidepressant, though it didn't

seem to help. That spring evening had felt cool and pleasant to her, but Michael had put on a sweater, saying he felt chilled. The moon had been bright in a clear sky. But sitting in the shadow of the roof, Michael had looked pale.

And now she was here, on a sunny morning, with this robust cousin of Michael's. His bronzed, handsome face looked quite well, or as Lizzie had said…

Healthy.

She rose from the chair, poured a cup of coffee and returned to her seat. He did the same and they sat at the table, out of the sun's glare, facing the banister. "I wouldn't tell him you weren't all right," he said with meaning. "Regardless."

Apparently Michael was in more trouble than just having to make some decisions. "Is there any way I can help him? Forget that. Apparently he doesn't want my help."

"Sometimes," he said quietly, "it's only between a person and God."

She nodded. "Right. Only I could decide about my relationship with Michael. But I don't have to leave home to make that decision." In the silence she came to another conclusion. "This isn't just about me, is it?"

She didn't bother to look at him. Her cup was half empty. So was she. Apparently, Noah wasn't going to reveal the secret life of Michael Nansen. "Okay, you said you would talk to me about your doorstep." She looked over at his face, seeing his troubled brow. "Is this Michael's house or not?"

"Not. It belonged to his mother. She and her new husband are moving to Charleston. She sold her part of the business to my dad. Dad bought this house, and I'm buying it from him."

Okay, number two. Wealthy?

"I'm thinking of getting rid of the contemporary furniture and restoring the house to its historic past."

Before thinking, she blurted, "Really? Michael and I discussed that. This house would be so perfect with period furnishings." When she and Michael had discussed this house, she'd been the one to point out its historical significance. Michael had preferred contemporary furniture.

"My thoughts exactly." Noah hunched over the table, toward her. "I'm planning to get my grandmother's period furniture out of storage. You…?" He leaned back again as if thinking he'd been too forward. "You have a knowledge of furnishings, too?"

Her heart leapt. She'd almost forgotten some of her dreams. "Interior design was my major in college. My minor was history."

"So you're into design and too?"

"Only…in talking about it." The warmth she felt was not from the sun, but from that inner self-consciousness. She'd thought about a lot since Michael left. Thought about the past. Thought about the future.

His lips parted as if he were about to question, like his eyes were doing. He seemed to think better of it and picked up his cup and drank from it, peering at her over the rim. His quizzical brow encouraged her to explain.

"I led tours during the summer of my senior year in college. Savannah's history fascinates me." She took a deep breath, remembering. Michael Nansen had fascinated her. The moment he'd walked into her senior history class, any other male had faded in comparison. He lit up a room like Lizzie had a way of doing. His hair was sunlight, his eyes the azure sky. His dimpled cheeks expressed his boyish charm.

He'd appealed to her aesthetic sensitivities. And yet, and yet, Michael seemed but a reasonable facsimile compared with this older, more serious, very handsome man, and she should not even be thinking that. Well, of course she should. She had artistic leanings. Symon had talked about that. He said a writer was generally more an observer than a participant in life. They noticed, they evaluated. That's all she was doing.

She expelled the breath she'd been holding. What had she

said aloud, and what were only thoughts? He was simply sitting, as if waiting, maybe…observing.

"Anyway," she said, "during senior break, Michael signed on as my assistant tour guide." He had said he could work at the family business, but he and Megan would never see each other that way. She would be working afternoons and evenings. He'd be working days. He'd wanted them to get to know each other better.

Now, she wondered if she'd really known him at all.

"After graduation, we both continued with that. Now, I might try and get into design. I've considered the idea of turning my house into a historic B and B, like my grandmother and I had discussed."

She hadn't meant to reveal so much about her and Michael. She'd hoped to discover something about the missing Michael. To escape Noah's studied gaze, she picked up her cup and stepped over to the pot for a refill. Returning to the table, she tried to lighten the mood. "The only things I've done with design in a long, long time is shift my furniture around, then move it back again."

An expected laugh or accommodating smile didn't come from him. Instead, he spoke seriously and his blue eyes sparked with a glint of the morning sun. "Since you have knowledge of interior design, and you're thinking about trying your hand at it, maybe you could give me some pointers on what to do with my period furniture."

He must have detected her surprise. Her open mouth might be a good indication. "I mean," he said, "on a professional level, of course."

"A…job?"

"If it wouldn't be…" He turned his face toward the wall, indicating the inside of the house. "Too personal."

Too personal? It took a moment for her to realize he meant because of Michael. But no. Replacing the contemporary with period furniture would just be another step toward removing

Michael from her memories, which she needed to do. He was gone. And regardless of his reasons, he hadn't included her, hadn't confided in her. She needed to stop thinking about him. Get on with her life.

She removed her gaze from Noah's hopeful eyes and the slightly lifted brows, awaiting her answer. She'd offered advice to friends on occasion, and they knew she had a special knack for decorating, particularly at Christmas. Annabelle and Symon had even incorporated some of her ideas about decorating for their wedding.

She couldn't say she'd be glad to help him as a friend. He wasn't a friend. He was a...what? Reminder of Michael?

His suggestion appealed to her. But, having heard about a heartbroken person's being on the rebound, or vulnerable, she wasn't sure taking him up on his offer would be...wise.

Chapter 5

When he arrived at the office on Monday morning, the office manager turned her curly gray head from the coffee table and said, "Good morning, Noah," in a way that made Noah wonder what delightful secret she had. Her eyes and her smile appeared more animated than usual. She'd been his dad's secretary for as long he could remember. And most of the years she'd worked there, she'd run the office. She'd tried to run him and Michael, also, when they worked on construction during summers between high school and college semesters.

He walked over. "Morning, Miss Jane. Can I help you with this?"

She swatted his arm. "I've been making coffee for this office longer than you've been living. And no man is going to take this job away from me."

He got the idea. "Then pour me a cup when it's ready, will you, please?"

"If you're still here," she said with a sly look. "Your dad wants to see you."

Uh-oh. What had he done now? He'd tried to get back into the swing of things during the past six months. He'd been more comfortable with a hammer in his hand than in the office. But he'd do what was needed. He finally moved out of his parents' house and into the one he'd just bought. Maybe his dad had another construction job for him to supervise, or maybe he wanted him to get the rest of his boxes out of the basement. Those were mainly things he'd packed up years ago before going into the military.

His dad lifted his head of prematurely white hair and handed Noah a memo sheet with a message on it. "Looks like that writer fellow wants to see you."

"Rider fellow?" Noah was trying to think if he meant horses or what. Nobody had ridden in the car with him.

"You know, those books you got me into reading. He called this morning. Wants you to come out to Miz Brandley's when you have time. I assured him you'd have time this morning."

Noah took the pink memo and looked at the name and number. "Sure. I'll call right away."

"You know where he lives?"

"Miz Brandley is Miss B, right?"

His dad nodded. "We've done some work for her in years past. That writer was the caretaker's son. Now he's famous." His dad nodded and smiled like he was pleased. "His dad really knew his business. Kept that mansion and property looking like a painting. Anyway, this Symon said he's in the caretaker's cottage on her property. That's where he and his dad lived when he was young."

"Amazing," Noah said.

"That the boy became a writer?"

"Not that. You never know what a person could become." He looked around when Miss Jane came in with two cups of coffee. "Thank you," he said as he took them and handed one to his dad.

"Well," she said. "What less could I do for a person going

to do business with a famous author? I took that message, you know."

"You read his books?"

"Of course. He's a native son. And how could anybody resist a good murder mystery?" She gave him a look and strode out the door. He had a feeling she was into karate and eager to use it.

His dad wore a pleasant look on his face, the kind Miss Jane had a way of giving to people around her.

"So," his dad said, after a swallow of coffee. "What's amazing?"

Noah took a drink of his own coffee and sat in a nearby chair. "Last week I went into the bookstore to get his book. He took time to ask who I was and what I did, and then he asked for my card."

"You scratched his back and now he's gonna scratch yours."

Noah laughed. "Well, I like to think opportunities come through prayer."

"Sure. But God has funny ways of answering sometimes."

"True." And many different ways than funny. Noah's own prayers for safety had been answered by his being back in this beautiful city. He'd prayed with some who did not return to their homes. He hoped they were in their heavenly home. He didn't know how prayer was answered. People still had choices, and others became victims of somebody else's bullet or land mine. But he wouldn't dare start a day without asking for God to be with him.

"But," his dad said, with lifted brows, "like I said, we've done work for Miss B in the past. This writer fellow probably remembers us."

Noah thought if that were the case, the author would have asked his dad to come out, not Noah. How or why wasn't all that important. What the author wanted was the most important. And if he only wanted to know what Noah thought of his new book, that was okay, too. He was almost finished with it.

He downed his coffee, then went to his office and had Miss Jane put a call through to Symon Sinclair. Obviously, Sy De-Berry was only his pen name. After a short conversation, Noah jumped into one of their white vans with the Fairfax-Nansen logo on the sides and headed out to Miss B's.

Turning onto the property was like becoming a part of a picturesque landscape. Spanish moss hung from the live oaks lining the drive and bordering the wide expanse of lawn that looked like a smooth green carpet.

He appreciated the historic district and the pristine mani-cured landscape of the squares and Victory Drive. But this was beauty magnified. Green shrubs offered a perfect background for plants and flowers in full bloom. He doubted there was a dead leaf anywhere. Noah estimated that both the house and the caretaker's cottage on his left were built in the late 1700s or early 1800s.

He began to remember when he was here years ago. Yes, he now recalled helping put on a new roof one summer while he was still a college student. He'd thought it a beautiful place then, but now he could see it was a storybook setting. He ap-preciated everything more now, even each breath of air, having been so close to death. The caretaker had been in charge, mak-ing sure everything was handled properly and no damage was done to anything. Including a leaf of a plant. Noah laughed.

Now, he thought he'd seen Symon then, too. He hadn't thought much of it then, but now he recalled Symon was about his age. Had been on the swimming team. They hadn't been friends. He knew Symon looked familiar but thought that was because of his pictures on the backs of his books.

Neat.

Maybe Symon remembered him. Well, maybe not. Noah had been on top of the three-story structure with a hammer and a nail in his hand.

Seeing a black sports car parked beside the cottage, Noah

parked the van on the side of the driveway, past the lane lead-ing to the cottage.

His eyes surveyed the cottage flanked by large oaks and hickory trees. It looked nicer than many of the historic homes. Maybe there was some renovation to do inside. Or maybe Symon Sinclair was helping Miss B with something she wanted done. He sat for a moment to keep in mind that fixing a cabi-net door is just as important, maybe more so, than building a house for a famous person. *Always lead me to the job You want me to do,* he prayed.

He exited the van, aware that the landscaping around the cottage was as pristine as the rest of the property. A perfect picture of well-cared-for grounds. As soon as he stepped onto the porch the front screen door opened, making him feel as if his visit was favorably anticipated.

Noah wore slacks, a short-sleeved white shirt and a tie, wanting to give the impression he could conduct business and he could work. He hoped he looked like a balance between a businessman and a skilled worker.

The author held out his hand. "Good morning, Noah Fair-fax," he said, his smile friendly. "Symon here."

They shook hands and Noah smiled. "I think we maybe met years ago when we did some work on Miss B's house."

"Miss B." Symon's nod held understanding. "You must've been a student of hers."

"That's right."

"Come on in," Symon said and Noah followed him into the living room. "I'm glad you stopped by my book signing. I've been thinking about contacting your company, but after meet-ing you, I thought I'd ask for you personally."

"Thanks." He walked through the living room with Symon, trying to glimpse anything that might be a renovation proj-ect but thinking more about this famous author seeming like a regular guy.

"I'm about two-thirds through the book. You'd think my

serving in Iraq would mean a story wouldn't scare me, but I'm at the place where—"

His words stopped, along with his feet and his heart. Then his heart beat triple-time to make up for it. Symon walked into the kitchen. Noah held on to the door casing. A white long-haired cat approached and played "ring around the legs" with him while a golden retriever stood back watching. But that's not what had caused Noah's anxiety attack.

Sitting at the table was a red-headed man about his age and the three gorgeous women he'd seen in the restaurant at the mall. The beauty queen, the vibrant one and Megan.

All three women stared at him. Blue eyes. Green eyes. And chocolate eyes. No lips smiled.

All his hopes of a great job, or even a small one with Sy DeBerry, even for the fixing of a cabinet door, went down a hole in the floor where he wished he could go. Now he figured he hadn't been summoned here for a job.

At least not a material one. Maybe Megan had told her friends he'd stalked her. Now he remembered Megan said she called Miss B her aunt. He was going to be in the hot seat and answer for his actions. They might insist he answer for Michael's actions, too.

Lord, help me, he quickly prayed.

He recalled the Bible passage about the people asking the prophet Jeremiah to pray for them. Then the scripture said that ten years later the prayer was answered. How long would Noah have to wait?

These friends and the famous thriller-killer writer were going to…kill him. That would be the easy part. They'd tar and feather him first.

Chapter 6

Noah's face reminded Megan of Michael's when he'd been sick with the flu last Christmas and never seemed to fully recover. Had it not been that his platinum-colored hair was lighter than his face, she'd say he was white as a sheet.

His flickering glances from her to the others and back again indicated he didn't expect to see her there. His deep blue eyes looked almost black on that off-white face.

"Coffee?" Symon gestured to the pot and took a cup from the cabinet when Noah nodded. "Have a seat."

"Just—just black," Noah said and pulled out a chair at the round table. Symon poured his coffee and Megan thought Noah's hand shook when he reached for the handle. He didn't lift the cup. Symon introduced Annabelle, Lizzie and Paul.

Symon sat across from Noah. "Heard you make a mean breakfast."

"Yeah, well." He sort of mumbled and half smiled. Even looking pale and rather self-conscious, he was handsome. Michael's dimples had been cute. Noah's lines at his mouth were more like character marks. His demeanor now was certainly different from the confidence he displayed at their breakfast.

Feeling a little guilty about his discomfort, Megan decided to offer him a tad of relief. "That was a compliment," she said.

His glance at her seemed to imply she'd just saved his life.

Lizzie popped in, "At least send her home with a take-out box next time."

"Next—?" Megan's head snapped around and her gaze met the mischievous twinkle in her friend's green eyes. Megan doubted her reprimanding silent message had any influence on whatever went on in Lizzie's head.

Lizzie smiled innocently. Symon turned the conversation back to the business at hand. "Annabelle and I are considering some renovations to the cottage," he said. He looked over at Megan. "I asked Megan to sit in on our discussion since she knows about historic homes and has already offered some advice."

Megan watched the color returning to Noah's face as he seemed to relax. She glanced at Annabelle and Lizzie, who sat on each side of her. They focused on Noah.

They'd be watching his every move and listening to every word. They'd said Noah had acted like a pervert. Symon said he'd behaved like a really decent man that had checked on Megan and then fed her. But then, Symon was a writer and writers didn't think like normal people. He wrote about killer characters, yet he seemed to trust people.

When Symon had mentioned Fairfax-Nansen Construction and Renovations as a possibility for the renovations he and Annabelle had in mind, Megan had balked. But Symon said that might be the way to get some word about Michael. Her friends had convinced her that if Noah were nearby, they all could keep a closer eye on him. She'd expected them to say she should steer clear of Noah Fairfax, but they'd said if she were serious about getting into design, this might be a good place to start.

Now, Symon was saying, "What all does your company do?"

"Just about anything you need. Minor repairs, restoring historic homes or building new ones." He went into detail, giving examples, as if trying to prove his family's business was a worthy company.

Noah then related how he'd grown up with a hammer in his hand, not with toys but a real toolbox and instructions on how to hammer a nail into a real board. He'd worked with his dad during summers from the time he was twelve years old. Besides his personal experience, he began to expound on his university studies until Symon stopped him.

"I wasn't seeking your lifelong credentials." Symon laughed lightly, which seemed to dispel Noah's attempt to ensure he was capable of the project. "My dad wouldn't have had the company work on Miss B's house had it not been reputable. Annabelle and I are interested in adding on a couple rooms, but we don't want it to look like an add-on or disturb the landscape."

Noah was nodding. "That kind of work is our specialty here in Savannah. Could I take a look at the house?"

They all followed as Symon took him through the house and Noah inspected, knocked on wood and made comments. When they returned to the kitchen, confidence laced Noah's voice. "Not only can we make the rooms look like part of the original house, we can use some of the same types of materials that are in this one."

"Same?" Symon queried.

"Several decades ago, a company who appreciates historic structures as much as we do began buying those scheduled for demolition," Noah explained. "They were relocated and restored. Those not salvageable still had valuable materials that could be taken and used in other buildings, and we have access to them."

Megan heard the pride in his voice and watched him stroke the door casing as tenderly as if it were one of the pets lying side by side on the floor. She heard him talk about beams, trim, windows, doors and floorings that had been harvested and restored.

Her thoughts, however, went to the conversations she and Michael had had about restoration. But, she reminded herself, they hadn't gone as far as making any definite plans. Symon and Noah were talking business, about a project Symon and Annabelle wanted done. Her conversations with Michael had been more along the lines of general conversation.

The questions had been like which house had she preferred, the one on Jones Street or Michael's? What changes did she think might be made in the house? Did she prefer historic or contemporary? There had always been that "if" factor or the "maybe," or a vague hinting at a life they might have together. There had been no firm commitment from either. She had thought that was falling in love, getting to know each other. And then it was habit, and later it was accepted they were together, and then he was ill.

Megan felt mesmerized, watching Noah talk, seeing the resemblance to Michael. If Michael had stayed with the company, that might be him talking about restoration, working with her friends in this way. He could have fit in with them all so very well. And he had, until a few months ago. He'd said he didn't want to work with the company. He'd needed to get his life back on track.

Apparently, she was not part of that track.

Sometimes, however, she felt like she'd been run over by a train.

She didn't realize she was staring at the man who might have been Michael until their eyes met and she felt a shock. It seemed to be the same for him. His words stopped. She glanced at the others and decided they hadn't noticed. They were watching Noah as Annabelle asked a question, and Lizzie was in listening mode for the answer.

Megan turned to the table and began to gather the cups and

take them to the counter. While the others talked about the subject that she was supposed to have been so interested in, she rinsed the cups and put them into the dishwasher.

Even when the conversation turned to Megan's considering turning her house into a B and B, or Noah making changes in his house, she could hardly fathom that this conversation was taking place with this cousin of Michael's. She and Michael had talked about the possibility of her turning the house into a B and B. He hadn't asked her to marry him, but he had asked what changes she thought should be made in the Nansen house.

She already had ideas. Why not share them with this cousin? Was Michael ever coming back? If Noah was telling the truth, Michael's mother apparently didn't think Michael was coming back. She'd sold the house. Had Michael tried to buy it and been refused?

Why did everything seem to be working well for Noah, though it hadn't for Michael? She'd been attracted to Michael not only because of his good looks, but also because of his fun-loving nature. He'd had a rough time while in college, had married and then divorced and had been devastated. After a year of having wasted his life, as he called it, he'd returned to college and earned a business degree.

She admired him for taking control of his life, wanted to make it count for something. She'd identified with his heartache over his failed marriage. She'd seen that heartbreak in her dad when he'd lost her mom to cancer. But her dad had recovered, and he'd married again. She was able to encourage Michael about that.

A startling thought occurred. Had Michael and his wife decided to reunite? That could explain a lot. He might be reluctant to tell her. Or Loretta might have stipulated their getting back together meant he must never have any contact with Megan again.

Megan would be able to understand that. She could not be sorry that a marriage would be saved. Interrupting her thoughts, Symon drew her attention by standing and speaking to Noah. "Let's go outside and take a look."

Megan knew what that meant. Symon had said, and Paul had agreed, that they would not only discuss renovation and building, but also try and see what was going on with this cousin of Michael's. The three men left the kitchen to go out back.

"Mudd, SweetiePie," Symon called. The dog and cat went outside with them.

Megan knew Noah had given a good impression so she wasn't surprised when Lizzie said, "Quit pretending you're interested in dirty cups. Come sit down and listen to our opinion. After all, you did ask us to check him out."

Megan closed the dishwasher door and sat at the table.

Annabelle said, "I am favorably impressed, Megan."

"Weren't you also impressed with Michael?"

"I liked Michael. But, like you, I was concerned about whatever was troubling him, with his health or whatever." She paused. "I don't know if we should try and compare him with Michael. Noah is a different person."

Megan scoffed. "How can I help it? Michael was here one day, gone the next. Noah looks like him. He lives in Michael's house. He's living the life that Michael should be living." She lifted her hands helplessly. "He's even talking about the changes in his house Michael mentioned. Along with the discussion about a B and B."

"That's not so odd," Annabelle said. "You said he's Michael's cousin. Their family owns the company together. It would seem even stranger if Noah and Michael were entirely different."

"More than that," Lizzie said, and Megan was almost afraid of the honesty Lizzie often exhibited. "I'm sorry Michael is having problems. But you deserve more than a man who walks out on you without a word."

"We hadn't promised—"

Lizzie was shaking her head. "Doesn't matter. You'd been dating for a long time. You were there for him when he was sick. Now that I've seen Noah, I think of Michael as someone with potential, and it's as if Noah is the finished product." Her face brightened. "Like the historic homes. Noah is a renovated one."

After joining them in light laughter, not about the differences but at the way Lizzie had of expressing her opinions, Megan said, "You're talking about outward appearance. Yes, Noah seems more mature, a couple years older, knows and likes the renovating business, so of course he sounds good."

"Looks good, too."

"Michael did, too."

"Michael was cute as a bug's ear," Lizzie said, then scrunched her face. "Anybody ever seen a bug's ear? Do bugs have ears? Anyway, he was adorable. But Noah is…is…like a younger version of that guy in the movie, what was it, *Nights in Rodanthe?*"

"Richard Gere," Annabelle said. "Right. We watched that together."

"Yeah," Lizzie said. "Swoon."

"Okay." Megan called a stop to that with uplifted hands. "It's settled, Lizzie. You can have him."

"Yeah," Lizzie said. "That's what Annabelle said about Symon when he first came to town. We met, we talked, we became instant friends. But he wasn't interested in me otherwise. He just wanted information about pirates. Even Annabelle's throwaway, Wesley, didn't want me and I didn't want him. Besides, I see the thread that runs between people who are attracted to each other."

"Thread?"

"Yeah. It's kind of like a spiderweb, like the ones you see everywhere in the fall. They float past, wrap around everything. That's what it looks like. And I see that with Noah and—"

"No way," Megan protested. "I felt that invisible spiderweb when I first saw Michael. He enjoyed the attention of females for a while, but then he sought me out and we hit it off. Okay, Michael was adorable. Noah is more seriously handsome."

"Oh, he has those laugh lines. And that hair. My goodness."

"But I'm in no condition to think about any man—and certainly not one who resembles Michael."

"One of these days you'll see the difference," Lizzie said. "And I see that spiderweb coming from him and trying to wrap you up."

"You silly," Megan said. "He feels sorry for me. He thinks I'm pitiful. Why would he want a girl Michael threw away?"

Lizzie smiled. "Because he's smarter. And more serious. And mature. And—"

"Stop it, Lizzie. If he's so great, you go for him."

She shook her head. "Won't work. I don't have a clicky button."

"Clicky button?"

"You know, like on computers and such. You just click on what you want. I think humans have invisible ones and mine has malfunctioned. If I even have one. I've dated every available man on those Christian dating services. Either they don't click, or I don't click."

"Your day will come."

Lizzie sneered. "Right. When I'm too old to care. My young life is being wasted. I'm a waitress in a pirate café. Big whoop."

"Well," Megan said reflectively, "at least you weren't talking about maybe getting married to someone who up and left you."

Lizzie reached over and patted Megan's hand. "I know. I'm sorry. I just yakety yak too much. I should be feeling sorry for you. But we both can just tell the world we don't care and wither and die as old maids." She punctuated that with a nod of finality. "How's that?"

"Perfect," Megan said. "I'll just draw caricatures for Annabelle's books and cook breakfast for happily married people who stay in my home that I turn into a B and B."

"Right. And maybe I'll come over and cook pirate pancakes for them."

"You cook pirate pancakes?"

"I think I just started. Those would sell. I could make a million bucks and buy me a...oops! Forget that. We don't want a man now, do we?"

By that time Megan was laughing so hard she thought she probably could live happily ever after as long as Lizzie was around.

Chapter 7

"You had me worried for a moment," Noah said after they walked out onto the back deck, descended the steps and stood in the yard.

Symon and Paul looked at him for an explanation.

Tearing his eyes away from the enticing creek that flowed farther down and the mesmerizing sound of water rushing along as if it had a mission, Noah gave a short laugh. "I wasn't sure who you were referring to when you called to Mudd and SweetiePie when we left the house. Now I think I know." He extended his hand toward the golden retriever and white ball of fluff walking down the path in the midst of the flora and foliage beneath the hickories and live oaks laden with Spanish moss.

Looking again at Symon and Paul he saw their smiles.

Symon explained. "Mudd was rescued from a hurricane disaster," he said. "I named him Mudd because his coloring looks like the mud, or red clay I should say, that holds things together. He's been an adhesive for me when I've needed it."

Noah was nodding, thinking about his own times of need as Symon explained the cat. "SweetiePie belongs to Miss B. She was a comfort to her and Annabelle at a time of need, too."

"I get that," Noah said. "And I know you're probably concerned about my showing up after Michael left."

The two men looked as if that's exactly what they had in mind.

"You see, I may not be as effective as a pet."

Their pleasant looks seemed to know where he was heading.

"But I'm trying to be a help to Michael in his time of need. My adhesive, as you call it, is the Lord."

Symon's hand went up like a stop sign as Paul nodded. "I've come to that conclusion," Symon said, "thanks to Miss B and Annabelle."

Noah was glad to hear that. "Maybe I didn't go about things in the right way. But I've tried to explain to Megan about my spying on her. I have to keep Michael's confidence. It's not my place, anyway, to tell Megan what Michael should tell her. But," he lifted his palms as if to say he was open to scrutiny, "I will tell you anything you want to know about me."

"Don't know about that. Not sure I want to reciprocate," Symon said with a touch of humor in his voice. "However," he added on a serious note, "we don't want Megan hurt any more than she's already been."

Noah wondered if Symon was about to say his company could work on the cottage, but he didn't want him bothering Megan. "Maybe I remind her too much of Michael?"

Symon glanced at Paul, who seemed to absorb every word as if he were a deep thinker with an opinion others would respect. As if Symon's glance were an invitation, Paul spoke up. "I think that reminder might be a good thing," he said. "She has to face the fact that her relationship with Michael appears to be over or at least at a standstill. If she begins the B and B renovation of her house, that's moving on with her life."

Symon nodded.

Noah thought of Megan staring at him, then her abrupt glancing away, then her beginning to clear the table. What had she been thinking? That he resembled Michael but wasn't Michael? Noah recalled Michael saying he didn't really belong there, with those people.

Right now, Noah knew the feeling.

If Michael had played his cards right, he would be here and not Noah.

Maybe that's why he was so surprised when their conversation turned to one that seemed more friendly.

"Join us for our morning swims at the fitness center," Symon said. "Paul and I go most mornings."

"We were on the swim team." Paul looked toward Symon. "He took us to the championships many times."

"You did your part, too," Symon said with an appreciative glance at Paul, then returned his gaze to Noah.

"I'm no champion swimmer," Noah said. "But we might play underwater tackle football."

They laughed and Symon said, "We don't compete in the pool. Just get our exercise and enjoy the water and the fellowship."

The word *compete* gave Noah a moment of pause. Just a word could stir the emotions. Like Megan had mentioned, a word could bring on the feeling of loss or grief when you weren't expecting it.

Any other time, Noah would feel honored to be included with these two men. He wanted friends. He needed friends. But he had a strong feeling their purpose was to know him better, to be protectors for their friend Megan.

"What time?"

"Six a.m." Paul said.

Noah pursed his lips but nodded.

"Afterward," Symon added, "when we're invited, which is most mornings, we go to Miss B's for breakfast."

"She cooks for you?"

"Not exactly. Willamina does that, but the women gather 'round and talk about what goes into what." Symon shook his head, but a softness came into his eyes. "Annabelle insists on learning to cook, although we'll rely on Willamina a lot after we're married. Now," he said, "about this backyard. Noah?"

It took a moment for Noah to realize he'd lost his concentration. Something in the creek had caught his attention. His glance went to Symon and Paul, then back to the creek. "Are the dog and cat in the creek?"

"They're a team," Symon explained. "Used to be enemies, but after Annabelle and I became friends, so did they. And I think they do it for the exercise. Mudd has a bad leg. The swimming is easier on him than walking, but he's getting better."

Noah forced his attention back to the men. "You were talking about the backyard."

Symon nodded. "Let me get the women to come out." He took a step along the path then stopped. A small chuckle escaped his throat and he motioned.

Lizzie opened the screen door and the three women came out. This confirmed to Noah that they'd prearranged for Symon and Paul to talk with him without the women being present. Yes, he'd better mind his p's and q's.

Just as the women joined them in the yard, the dog and cat jumped out of the creek and began to shake. Noah gasped. They all followed his gaze and laughed. The cat was particularly weird looking. Its hair stuck out from its face like something wild. He'd never seen a cat with big blue eyes whose fur stuck out like splinters.

"Quite a sight," Noah said.

Annabelle laughed. "SweetiePie must be posing for Megan. She's making cat sketches for my book."

"You write books, too?"

"Not really. Just a story for children about a cat's bad hair day."

Noah was impressed that this beautiful woman seemed

to have a modest spirit. He suspected she was beautiful inside, too.

Symon put his arms around Annabelle's shoulders, and Noah felt the emotion. Just like a word could conjure up a bad feeling, a look into each other's eyes by two people in love could arouse a yearning for something like that of your own. Something that could be strong and permanent. He had to look away.

Symon said, "I've told her a short book for children is just as important as a thick thriller-killer novel."

"Not as many words," she said. "And mine is based on a true story."

Symon moved away, scowling. "You think a killer is more important than our own true story?"

"Nothing is more important than that." Annabelle moved to him and kissed his lips.

A gagging sound made Noah look at Lizzie, who had stuck her finger in her open mouth. "Would you two lovebirds like for us to leave, or do you want to talk business?"

Annabelle and Symon both raised their eyebrows. Then Symon lifted his hands in a helpless gesture. "I prefer the former, but since Noah came all the way out here, maybe we'd better talk business."

Noah listened carefully as Symon and Annabelle talked about enlarging the patio and adding a guest room and an enclosed, mainly glass porch with outside access to the patio.

Annabelle pointed to the spacious backyard at Miss B's house. "We can always use Aunt B's yard for any big gatherings."

"Yes," Symon said. "She's our family and included in most things. But Annabelle and I want our own private place for the two of us. And there will be times when I'll entertain my publisher and a few people in my profession for business purposes."

Noah nodded. "Of course. I can get blueprints and plans made up."

Symon added, "We've already talked to Megan about sketching out how it would look."

Noah wondered if he meant the two of them should work together. Probably not.

Noah would have all the statistics. His job would be the building of the enclosed porch and guest room. His company would have input on design and how everything would look in cooperation with the patio. Their company could hire any designers to make sure everything went together.

"You know I'm not a professional," Megan said, bringing Noah's attention from his thoughts and to her. "I'm sure they have designers who know where to place every item."

"Right," Symon said. "But your drawings will have the flesh on their skeletal depictions. And you bring to it that personal touch. Noah and his company don't know why the design has to include our being able to view a particular part of the creek."

While the others seemed to enjoy a moment of smiles and nods, Annabelle moved to him and put her arm around his waist.

"Oh, no," Lizzie moaned. "Here we go again." She leaned toward Noah and said conspiratorially, "Their private joke."

"Oh," Annabelle said, moving away from Symon. "Willamina's waving. That means 'come to lunch.'"

Noah looked up to the big antebellum mansion and the dark-skinned woman out on the patio motioning to them. "You know I don't like to be kept waiting," she called. "Now, come on up here. All of you."

Noah stuck out his hand toward Symon. "Been nice meeting with you all—"

Symon didn't extend his hand but shook his head. "When Willamina said 'all' she meant you, too. Aunt B said she's looking forward to seeing you again."

"Uh-oh," Noah said. "I hope I've outgrown her reprimands for acting up in class."

"Did you dare do that?" Paul asked as they began walking up the path toward the big house.

"Not really. We all loved her, respected her. Wanted to please her."

In grade school he'd thought her the smartest, finest person he'd ever known. In later years he knew her as the refined lady in the antebellum mansion whose dad had been a state senator. But she'd acted just as pleasant and was still beautiful when he was a college student working on her roof. What would she be like now? He still had the feeling he'd had in the classroom—wanting to please her.

Noah longed to be a part of a group like this, not on the outside being watched lest he hurt Megan like Michael had done. He longed to be in on that private joke all of them seemed to know. He longed to have someone special like Symon had. To have his own...

He breathed a sigh of relief as they reached the screen door and he dispensed with longing for what he didn't have. That became replaced with a longing for whatever aroma permeated the warm air, whetting his appetite for down-home cooking.

It beat military rations any day.

As soon as he stepped inside, Miss B came toward him, arms extended. "I'd know that hair anywhere."

He headed for her, delighting in this southern hospitality he'd missed so much.

At the same time, a thought nagged. Michael hadn't been taught by her. He'd missed a lot. Noah had more advantages—not monetarily but in other ways. A great advantage was having Miss B as a teacher.

If things had been different for Michael, he might be here now.

Was Megan wishing that Noah was Michael?

Noah wished...

No, he mustn't.

Chapter 8

A week after that meeting at Symon's cottage followed by lunch at Aunt B's, Megan got the phone call. Noah said he wanted to catch her before she went to work. The contemporary furniture had been removed and period furniture delivered.

"I don't think my pushing the furniture against the walls will do anything for the decor."

She'd made up her mind that when or if he called she would go to his house. She would not consider this a job but would give her opinion of where to set the pieces. Her main reason, though, was to come right out and ask him if Michael had gone back to his wife.

That's about the only thing that made any sense. "Yes, I can come in the morning. Nine o'clock?"

"Yes. Sure. That's…that's great."

His stammering meant he hadn't thought she'd do it. But it was settled. "See you in the morning." She hung up with a nod of finality at her phone, then went about her daily living, which included conducting a tour that afternoon.

On the trolley, she began the explanation as usual with the emphasis on the important role women had played in the preservation of Savannah's history. Moving on, she glanced at the college student learning to become her assistant and remembered that Michael had charmed her bosses into letting him be her assistant. Then he'd charmed the tourists, and she'd loved it.

Such thoughts were not allowed, and a renewed sense of determination swept over her as they neared the heart of the historic district and the birthplace and childhood home of Juliette Gordon Low. "She was the founder of the Girl Scouts in the USA," Megan said, being reminded of what one woman could accomplish. And Megan liked to throw in a question now and then. "Anyone know her nickname? What she was called by her family and friends?"

Only once had a tourist answered that correctly.

Today, no one knew.

"Daisy." When Megan gave the answer they smiled at that personal bit of information.

"The house is Regency architecture, built somewhere between 1818 to 1821," Megan stated with a sense of pride. "It's now owned by the National Girl Scout Organization. It contains many of the original furnishings of the Gordon family."

Just the mention each night of the important role women played in the history of Savannah and the preservation of it boosted her spirits. She also knew that Mrs. Low had sketched, and had became a noted painter. If women could do things like that, Megan Conley could certainly survive the abandonment of Michael Nansen.

Late that evening she passed the house Noah now lived in and saw that light seemed to stream from every window. She had noticed large vans parked there when she'd passed by on a few mornings.

Had Michael still lived there, she would stop and ask, "What in the world are you doing?" Or she would stop to see how he was feeling.

Now, she continued on and parked at the back of her house, exited the car and deliberately turned her thoughts to the fragrant scent of flowers and evergreens in the full bloom of summer. The breeze cooled the humid air, which would make for a good night's sleep with her upstairs windows open.

Walking up the steps onto the deck, she prided herself on how well she was doing at pushing Michael out of her mind. After all, if a guy didn't want her, she certainly didn't want him. That's all the thought she needed to give that. She was getting on with her life. Doing well.

And she didn't have to worry about his having become more ill. Likely, he had returned to his wife. Megan could live with that.

She opened the screen, pushed the key into the lock, turned the knob and walked inside. Upon closing the door behind her, she faced the silent, dark house. Awash with memories, she stepped to the kitchen doorway. The late-evening light lay against the windows, unable to invade the darkness. The air was stale and warm. There was no aroma of freshly baked cookies. No offer of hot chocolate when the weather turned cold. No tinkle of ice splashed into a glass of sweet tea on a summer night. No precious words of greeting from a woman trying to regain control of her speech after a stroke.

No Grandmother.

But that was all right, too. Her grandmother had never completely recovered, and after having that second stroke she did not like having to stay in the nursing facility. But she'd handled it with great faith and endurance and now she was in her heavenly home, well and happy.

Megan reached inside the doorway and flipped the switch, flooding the room with light and forcing herself to smile at the memories. There were so many good ones. That's what Grandmother would want her to focus on. Grandmother would say,

"You're young. You have your life ahead of you. Make the best of it." That's what Aunt B would say, too. And her friends.

Yes, she thought, turning into the hallway. Stepping into the dark patch juxtaposed against the light on the hardwood floor of the hallway she thought of Annabelle, who had lived here with her and Lizzie during three years of college and the year and several months after their graduation. She missed her friend's beautiful face and smile. She thought of Annabelle's heart, even lovelier than her outer appearance.

Glancing at the closed door of the room that had been Annabelle's, she felt the urge to open it. How nice it would be to hear the delightful sound of, "Hey, you're home. Get your jammies on and let's talk." And during the past few months that had been primarily about Symon.

Megan thought it wonderful that Annabelle had fallen in love with Symon. She'd been absolutely transformed from contentment to pure joy. And Megan understood Annabelle's moving in with Aunt B so they could plan the wedding and she could be nearer to Symon to plan their future together.

Lizzie's door was open, but she was working at the Pirate's Cave until around ten and then she had a date. The nights when she was home, she'd do something like stick her head of red hair out the door, then duck behind it, hold out an empty bottle and say, "Hey, I used the last of your shampoo for you. Say thank you." Or something equally profound.

She felt herself smile as she switched on the light in her room. At least she still had Lizzie here.

As long as Grandmother had been alive, even in the nursing home, this had still felt like her grandmother's house.

Now it was Megan's. The more she thought of it, the more she wanted to turn it into the B and B like her grandmother had talked about doing before she had the stroke. Grandmother had said Megan would marry and move out one of those days. Ironically, it had been both her grandmother and the man Megan had thought about marrying who left.

But no, Megan was not going to think about that. Instead, she thought about the changes that would be made in her own life if she turned this house into a B and B. She and Lizzie could still live here. Or Aunt B had offered to let them both live with her.

Megan wasn't sure what to do. But at least she was thinking about her future—on her own like an adult. Although she liked conducting the tours, it was not what she wanted to do for the rest of her life.

She had a full life and began to realize how much time and thought she'd put into worrying about Michael, spending time with him, hoping he'd regain his health and be the wonderful guy she'd told herself he was. She wasn't sure anymore what was truth and what had been her idealized version of him. But she was making decisions now on how to make progress in her life and not just spin her wheels.

Maybe by the time she showered and got into her pjs, Lizzie would be home. The time she came home depended on how things went on her date.

After drying her hair and getting into her pajamas, Megan opened her windows and decided to settle in bed for her devotional time. Just then, the back door slammed. That said a lot about how her friend's date had gone.

Sure enough, by the time Megan got to her doorway, Lizzie wailed, "Let me wash that guy off my hands, then I'll tell you all about it."

Megan went to the kitchen, got a Coke from the refrigerator and poured some for them.

"This one," Lizzie said on her way into the room, "has won three hamburger eating contests and has the belly to prove it." She pulled out a stool at the island and plopped onto it. After a sip of her soda, she slumped. "Why do they send me guys like that?"

"Because you ask for it," Megan said.

"I don't ask for bellies bulging with burgers. I want a nice

Christian fellow looking for a...a...girl like me." She brushed her hair back from her face with her fingers. "Is that the problem?" Her green eyes widened. "They see my picture and think that's the kind of guy I want?" Moaning, she added, "None of them suit me."

Megan could say sincerely, "None can come up to your worth, Lizzie. That's the problem. They're single guys looking for a girl."

Lizzie took on her deflated look. "I guess they're as desperate as me. Maybe I should settle—"

"Don't you dare, girl. The right man for you is out there. He just hasn't come along yet."

"Okay, you convinced me." She lifted her glass. "In the meantime, you and I have each other."

Megan clinked her glass to Lizzie's. "Exactly," she said. But there was one difference between them. Lizzie wanted to find Mr. Right. But Megan felt rather trampled on by the last man in her life and as far as she was concerned right now, he could very well be the last one. Her life didn't depend on whether or not a man was in it.

And to punctuate that, after retiring to her room, she thought only about the way she would handle things in the morning when she went to Michael's...no...Noah's house.

During the past two weeks, she'd seen the progress that the construction company was making on the cottage. The additional rooms would be on the side, nearer the trees and closer to the creek. She learned that Noah was not doing the construction work himself, but each morning after his swim with Symon and Paul, and the breakfast at Aunt B's, he supervised their work. She was told he sometimes picked up a hammer himself.

She got into bed and reached for her devotional book. After the reading, she switched off the lamp, took a deep breath of the cool night air, then settled in for her prayers. She usually fell asleep while praying and wondered if God invented prayer to help people sleep better. Worked for her.

Only for an instant did her mind wander to Noah Fairfax, who seemed to have a penchant for prayer.

And tomorrow morning, like a perfectly capable adult woman, she would see Noah Fairfax, ignore his resemblance to that other man and conduct her business without any problem.

She nodded against the pillow as if raising her glass in a toast, and this time it was she who counseled herself. "Okay, you convinced me."

Chapter 9

That's what Megan kept telling herself the next morning while deciding what to wear at her meeting with Noah Fairfax. She was not accustomed to such uncertainty. It seemed she'd become a different person since Michael had left.

Okay, all she needed to do was think clearly.

She wasn't trying to impress anyone so casual jeans and a knit shirt or silk blouse would do.

On second thought, on looking into the closet of clothes she hadn't worn in a long time she gave herself that talk again about moving on with her life. And clothes had something to do with it. Annabelle's working with the modeling studio meant Megan and Lizzie had received first-hand instruction on style. Annabelle, being a public person, felt required to dress accordingly most of the time and her friends couldn't run around with her looking like a grunge. They'd enjoyed dressing up and going out when Annabelle was with Wesley, Megan with Michael and sometimes Lizzie with one of her dating-service guys.

This was different. A midmorning…what?

Noah Fairfax was a supervisor with a well-known renovation company, and he was asking for her input on interior decorating. Maybe he just felt sorry for her. Or maybe he really was trying to help with Michael's problem. He said he wanted to help her, too.

Well, she didn't need any help, she told herself again as she chose her clothes from the closet. She slipped into a denim pencil skirt and topped it off with a stretch cotton wing-collar blouse. She brushed her naturally wavy hair until it fell softly around her shoulders, pulled a few tresses out from her face and lightly sprayed.

After applying melon color to her lips she tucked her feet into red patent-leather three-inch wedge-heeled sandals.

"There," she said, looking approvingly at her reflection as she fastened gold loop earrings. That should be enough to show she could be on her way to becoming a consultant or interior designer whether or not the Fairfax-Nansen company might need one.

She liked looking the part of a businesswoman. After all, she was owner of this house and had a hefty bank account, thanks to her grandmother. Therefore, she was not just some abandoned girl who wallowed in the failings of her past. She would learn from her history and look forward to the future. She would not even think about Michael's cousin…but might even consider Noah Fairfax's company to convert her home into a B and B.

Or not.

She was in control of her life and would act accordingly. No man would dominate her thinking ever again. Looking back, she realized that Michael and his needs had dominated for a long time. But Grandmother's needs had dominated at one time, and that's how it should be. Isn't that what was supposed to happen with family and friends and loved ones?

Hearing the determined click of her heels along the hardwood hallway, she reminded herself anew that she was a woman in charge of her life—under God, of course—and was ready to act accordingly.

"Woo-hoo," Lizzie said upon her entry into the kitchen. "He's going to think you're the cat's meow."

Megan huffed. "That's not my purpose, Lizzie. I'm going there on business, so I'm trying to look the part."

"You look great, of course, but I haven't seen you dressed up since—"

Megan scoffed. "Since church yesterday?"

Lizzie lifted her hands and gazed toward the ceiling and back again. "I mean everyday. You've been such a grunge until you get into that tour uniform."

"You're one to talk. Look at you. Still in your nightclothes. And everybody in Savannah, Georgia thinks you're a real pirate, the way you dress all the time."

"Touché," Lizzie said, then grinned. "But it's good to see you looking almost human again." She tried to push her hair back from her face but her fingers got tangled in its wild disarray.

Megan laughed, then thanked her for the cup of coffee she took from the one-cup machine. She hoped she'd never take for granted the friendship she had with Annabelle, Lizzie and Aunt B. They did take for granted to a certain extent that they loved each other and could say anything and mean it for the other person's good, and when they disagreed they accepted the others' opinions.

Never before had it entered her mind that friends might have a falling out or one might be deserted by another. Never...until Michael disappeared.

She did not like negative thinking. She refused to do that today.

"This is the first day of the rest of my life," she said, quoting the adage.

"Really?" Lizzie pondered. "I think it's my..." She touched

her cheek with her index finger. "Maybe my twenty-fifth year. Oh!" She grimaced. "Do you know we're a quarter of a century old?"

"Thanks," Megan said. "You're making my day."

Lizzie grinned, then sobered. "Want me to go with you?"

Megan glanced at the wall clock. "The meeting's at nine. I wouldn't want you to outshine me in those skimpy pjs." She finished her coffee. "Anyway, this is a one-on-one kind of thing."

"Keep your chin up." Lizzie grinned. "And remember, when you get back, we'll go to Aunt B's for lunch and to discuss wedding plans."

Megan nodded, then hurriedly went to brush her teeth one more time and apply the melon gloss again. Eyeing herself carefully in the mirror, she decided she made an all-right appearance of a casual-dressy person who didn't expect a lot and yet was prepared for whatever may come.

She told Lizzie she'd decided to walk the couple blocks and around the corner to Mich…Noah's house.

"In the meantime, I'll get dressed," Lizzie said. "Just call when you're ready to leave and I'll pick you up."

She'd become accustomed to exhaust fumes, trolley noise, the closeness of tourists, thinking about speaking clearly and distinctly, and watching guests for any sense of boredom. Now she was grateful for the freedom that came from breathing the fragrant morning air beneath a clear blue sky, walking along the brick sidewalk, appreciating the pristine boxwoods and evergreens and the Spanish moss-laden live oaks and hickories. The brisk walk was invigorating.

Yes, she had much to be thankful for. This was a new day and she had a lifetime ahead of her. Nearing the house, she told herself she would not go in the back way or have breakfast on the deck as if Noah were picking up where Michael left off.

She rolled her eyes. Michael had never done that. But Megan's interaction, if there was to be any, was going to be strictly on a business level. She would pretend to trust Noah. Okay, so Michael, according to Noah, wanted a report on how Megan was doing without him. Very well. Noah could report that she was A1, top-notch, just fine, not falling to pieces, or however he wanted to express it.

She refused to hesitate at the bottom of the curved steps. She lifted her red patent-leather-sandaled foot from the brick sidewalk onto the first step. She looked at and appreciated the green plant that grew underneath and along the sides, giving the impression one was walking along a path of white stepping stones in a field of ivy.

Megan lightly touched the curved iron railing, reminiscent of both the Federalist and English Regency styles, as she ascended the steps and then stood on the balcony bordered by the iron railing. She started to touch the ornate knocker but noticed the bell, so she rang it.

She thought it was taking a while for him to answer. Perhaps he expected her at the back. Then she heard the sound of the knob turn and the wood door opened. There was no screen to separate them at the front. He was right there, with his platinum hair and that look in his eyes that her friends described as kindness. She got the impression it was perhaps sympathy.

She didn't need that.

She looked away from whatever was in his blue eyes, a shade darker than Michael's, a shade darker than the sky but just as clear.

"Good morning," he said. "Please come in."

"Thank you." She stepped inside as he moved away for her to enter. She saw it then. The room was no longer furnished with Michael's contemporary furniture; it was filled with antique furniture in disarray.

She took a very deep breath and detected the odor of items that had likely been stored for a while.

"What am I to do with this?" he said, drawing her attention back to him.

She did not want to look at his face, his hair or his eyes, so her glance skirted toward him and then around the room. "I think that's why I'm here."

That was supposed to sound playful, but she heard the discomfort in her tone, the forced words. She would simply look around for a while, so she moved to touch a couch with its beautiful pattern and tried to focus on it. For some strange reason it seemed blurry.

Maybe it was the pattern, the color, the clutter or her eyes adjusting to coming from the sunlight into the dimmer room— or maybe it was germ infested from whatever had made Michael sick. She felt sick.

"Would you like something to drink?" he said, as if he noticed something was wrong.

Nothing was wrong. "No. I'm just thinking."

"All right," he said slowly and she turned her face away from him lest she appear as pasty as she felt. "Like it's been mentioned a few times…"

Yes, this had been mentioned. First at breakfast on the back porch, another time at the cottage and later at Aunt B's before the appointment had been made for her to give her opinion of what he might do with the interior to give it historic significance.

Her mind didn't seem to be working and she feared her knees were going to stop holding her up. She felt weak.

She saw him move, and he said, "Let's go in the kitchen, have something to drink, sit at the table and discuss this mess." She heard his attempt at a small laugh. Was it about the mess. Or…her?

Unsure what else to do, she followed the blur ahead of her.

She and Michael had gone through the house. He'd asked what she would do if the house were hers. She'd read too much into that, apparently.

She tried not to, but she thought of Michael. And missed him—or at least the man she thought he was. He'd been appealing, smart, fun. Now he was a man with a past he was trying to deal with. Had she really known him at all? What had she been to him?

Who was Michael?

Where was Michael?

Why was this man here?

What was this all about?

She missed her grandmother.

And she felt it coming. Like an overwhelming sweep of an ocean wave she'd seen at Tybee Island.

Her control was going.

One single sob came from her throat and then the waterworks began. He stepped into the kitchen, but she trudged past him and stumbled down the hallway to the back door.

He said her name, but she shook her head. Or was it her whole body shaking? She lifted a limp hand to ward him off. If he, or anyone in the whole world, touched her, she would crumble.

She might anyway. She opened the wooden door, then the screen and stepped out. He was right there, standing in her way and preventing her from going down the steps. She bumped into him as they both reached for the chair to pull it out from the table.

His hand gripped her arm. "Just sit," he commanded and she was too helpless not to obey.

She dropped her tote bag, sat and laid her head on her arms on the table.

And then she crumbled.

Chapter 10

Noah stood helplessly, his hands making fists then his fingers stretching as if in some kind of exercise program. That mimicked his feelings of helplessness. Do this, do that—he had no idea.

She mumbled something.

"Mitote?" He tried to mimic the word she'd said.

"Tote," she said. She sniffed and lifted her head enough to put her hand over her mouth and nose, but he managed to make out her words. "My bag."

"Oh, here it is." It was a couple feet away. Glad to have something to do, he held it out to her free hand.

Her shoulders lifted with each intake of air and her eyes kept blinking as she delved into the bag and came out with a napkin. She looked at it and moaned, tossed it onto the table and laid her head on her arms again.

"Go away," she said.

"If you promise not to move."

"I c-can't."

He didn't know if she meant she couldn't promise or she couldn't move. But he'd chance it. He went inside and immediately returned. "Here. Try this."

She sat upright, took what he held out to her, used it, then blinked to dry her eyes while taking in great gulps of air. She was trying to say something. He hoped she would confide in him, let him console her, reassure her, although he felt totally inadequate. He pulled out a chair and sat opposite her, waiting.

She held out the wad in her hand. "This is a table napkin." She sounded like someone with a very bad head cold. "Not a handkerchief."

"It was either that or the tablecloth." He pointed to the discarded napkin. "Since you didn't use this, I didn't think a paper towel would be in order."

She attempted to laugh despite the waterfall flowing down her cheeks. "That's—"

She pointed and he lifted a fold of the paper napkin with the tip of his finger. Then he saw a familiar face. He opened it. "It's SweetiePie." He wanted to laugh at the caricature, but he was uncertain how she might take that. He stifled it and said, "That's what she looked like when she came out of Symon's creek and shook. Strange sight, seeing her and Mudd in the creek like that."

Megan nodded. "That's why Annabelle wants to write about SweediePie and Budd. They used to be enemies."

He put his hand to his lips to keep from smiling at her attempt to make herself clear with a stuffy nose.

After sniffing and taking a deep breath she tried again. "That was the day Symon and Annabelle fell in the creek. The cat and dog became friends. The moral of Annabelle's story is that it's much better to accept the differences in animals—or people—instead of judging by how they look."

"Must be something special in that creek," he said and grinned, wondering if he might take Megan and jump in the creek with her. He didn't like to think they might be "end-emies."

His grin faded, however, when her breath came faster. He hoped she wouldn't hyperventilate. He wasn't sure if that would call for a paper bag to breathe into or resuscitation of a different kind. No, the latter was probably confined to the creek. He couldn't help but laugh at the thought as he looked at the sketch.

She shook her head. "That's probably how I look right now."

"Oh," he began and felt the words stop in his throat. He'd been about to say, "Far from it," and it seemed the words in his mind fell over each other about what a beautiful woman she was and all the qualities he admired about her and if she were not so much in love with Michael… Fortunately, the words piled up in his mind and he realized he should never, ever say them—not even think them. He didn't really think them. They just happened to trip across his brain, unbidden.

Her storm had lessened to a light rain that now dribbled down her cheeks. Her voice squeaked. "I don't know why I did that."

"I don't know how you couldn't," he replied sincerely. "This is the first time you've been in there since he left, isn't it? There must be a lot of mem—"

"No," she said as the dribble increased. He might have to bring out a few more napkins. "There are no great memories of being in the house," she said, which seemed odd to him. "I mean, we have been in there, talked about the house, even sat at the kitchen table and ate a sandwich one time, but we didn't spend much time here. He really hadn't been feeling well since Christmas. Also, I have accountability friends. And Aunt B to answer to."

Suddenly she moaned. "Oh, that didn't come out right. It sounds like without friends, or someone keeping tabs on me, I'd—"

"No," he said, feeling she was even more wonderful by the

moment. "Not at all. I'm well aware of the standards you and your friends have." He thought he'd better soften that, in case. "But anyone can make a mistake. I guess we all do. But we have a heavenly Father who forgives when we ask."

She shook her head and he understood her mumble this time when she said, "What am I doing?" And he knew she wasn't asking him, but herself. She reached for the SweetiePie sketch and folded it, then returned it to her tote.

He realized she had a tender heart. At times she'd been aloof and he couldn't blame her, but now he felt she'd just been bearing up under her loss. That wasn't easy. He'd been there, done that. Maybe he should let her know.

"You're expressing emotion," he said. "Something we guys are not supposed to do." He could feel it now but sure hoped he wouldn't. He hadn't cried when he saw his buddies blown apart. Or when they took a bullet. The living ones just went through the motions of their training and did what needed to be done. They had to keep their eyes open and their wits about them and simply be soldiers.

But after coming home, he'd drowned his sobs in a pillow many nights and at other times in the shower, always having music or television or noise in the background. But he didn't want to say anything that might make her compare her loss of Michael with the loss of life on the battlefield.

A heartache was not something to be compared or diminished. Everyone had a right to grieve over any kind of hurt or disappointment.

"I don't want you telling Michael that I'm falling apart," she said. "That's not it at all. I think seeing his furniture gone reminded me that he is gone. It's like when I got the call about my grandmother."

She was looking beyond him and he dared not look directly at her, lest she decide not to confide in him. She was trying to explain, redeem herself in her eyes.

"I closed my phone as Lizzie walked into the room. She

asked what was wrong but I couldn't speak. She did it for me and asked if it was about grandmother. I tried to make my lips move but they only trembled."

Noah saw fresh tears appear in her eyes. "I couldn't even say that Grandmother had died. It wasn't unexpected. I thought I could deal with it, knowing that she was better off and in heaven."

He nodded. "I understand. I've had times of believing I was handling things all right, too. But I wasn't here for…the funeral." Maybe identifying with Megan's emotion is what made him feel emotional. He thought that was over and done, too. He looked down at the table, preferring to forget but remembering anyway. He wanted Megan to know he knew about loss. "I haven't talked with anyone about this," he said, "but now I realize I need to."

Megan cleared her throat. "Whose…funeral?" she asked.

He took a deep breath and exhaled. "Loretta's," he said. "I didn't think I'd do it, but I cried much like you're doing when I went to the graveyard where she's buried. I even sobbed aloud."

He felt the silence. The stillness. Finally when he looked across at Megan, her eyes had dried but widened. Her mouth was open. She looked stunned.

"Michael's Loretta?" she said in an astounded whisper.

Her actions made Noah sit at attention. What had Michael told her? Or not told her?

He gave a quick nod.

Her next question totally astounded him. Her words were strangled, struggling to escape her throat. "She…died?"

Chapter 11

Megan stared at Noah. His eyes darkened. His face paled.

She held her breath, waiting for an answer that did not come. But hadn't he already acknowledged that Loretta had died?

Noah's eyes closed for a moment, then he lifted his chin and breathed the words, "Oh, Lord."

She thought that was really a prayer and he hadn't meant to say it aloud. He rose from the chair and went inside.

Why?

Was he crying?

Why had Noah said Michael's Loretta had died and Noah had cried aloud at her grave?

Well, of course, he cried because he cared. Megan's friends had cried with her after her grandmother died. That had been their way of relating to Megan, caring about her loss. They cried even though Grandmother had lived a full life and was ready to meet her Lord.

What were the secrets Noah and Michael shared? Why had Michael said he was divorced if Loretta, in fact, had died?

How did she die?

Who was telling the truth? Michael or Noah?

What was the truth?

Confusion continued to pile up. Instead of getting more answers from Noah, she thought of more questions.

If Loretta had died, then her assumption that Michael had reunited with her was all wrong.

Megan reached for her tote, then remembered her emergency makeup was in her purse, which she'd left at home. She scoffed at how she'd planned to make a professional appearance. Instead, she'd shown her lack of control over her emotions. And no telling what her tear-soaked face looked like. Probably a clown's with mascara streaks.

Sure enough, when she wiped beneath her eyes it left black streaks on the napkin. Now, she felt rather ridiculous about having displayed such unrestrained emotion.

Michael's leaving without saying goodbye or giving a reason was a blessing because it happened before their relationship had become more serious. She knew that. But it hadn't kept the tears from falling. What had she cried about anyway?

Fumbling in her tote, she found her phone and punched the buttons. "Pick me up when you can," she said when Lizzie answered. "And please bring my purse that's on my bedside table. I didn't put it in my tote."

"Sure. See you in a jiff."

She dropped the phone back into the tote and clutched the cloth napkin just in case the deluge began again.

She didn't look around upon hearing the screen door open. A cup of creamy coffee was set in front of her and Noah returned to the seat across from her with his cup.

He didn't say anything else, so she didn't, either, after looking at the starkness of his face. She couldn't put the pieces of the puzzle together. Had Loretta died after the divorce?

Her breath caught when she wondered what else Michael hadn't told her. She had to take in a few more gulps of air before she could ask, "Did Michael and Loretta live in this house together? Did she…" her voice became a whisper. "Did she die in there?"

"No," Noah said quickly. "Michael had an apartment. His mother lived here until she remarried and then Michael moved in here and returned to college. Or," he said, "that's my understanding of it."

She nodded. "That's what he told me."

She knew Noah wouldn't answer, but somehow the question escaped her throat. "Was he…leading me on? Just giving the impression he wanted a future with me?"

Noah's brow furrowed as he looked at his coffee but didn't pick up his cup. Then he glanced out at the backyard and simply shook his head.

No, he couldn't answer that.

Neither could she.

And she did not like the impression forming in her mind.

At the same time, she didn't want Noah or anyone turning this into some kind of drama. By becoming unglued, she'd negated any prospect of relating with Noah on a professional level, so she might as well make clear there was no need to relate on any other level.

"I'm not heartbroken," she said. "He never asked me to marry him. Our conversations were about changes, which house I liked better, if I wanted children, what I wanted in a man."

"Do you want to share your answers?" Noah asked.

"No," she said quickly. "I simply want closure on this and that's what I'm doing right now. I realize I've put an end to you and me relating on a professional level. I want to put an end to talking about Michael. If he ever has anything to say to me, he can do so and I may or may not listen." She nodded, punctuating that.

"I beg to disagree. We haven't even begun to relate on a

professional level, and after seeing the SweetiePie sketch, I'm more intrigued than ever about your artistic ability."

A tiny smile curved his lips and narrowed his eyes, which held a hint of humor. Then he said, "Let's pray about it."

Before she could say she often prayed about God's will in her life, he bent his head and closed his eyes. With bowed head she watched him as he talked to God as if He were sitting there. "Help us know what is right and good and seek your will, Father," he prayed. "You know what is in our best interest and we ask now for your guidance. Help us to listen and obey. Give us wisdom, Lord. Keep Michael and Megan in your care. Bless them. Give them peace. In Jesus' name, amen."

Instead of this being encouraging, Megan felt inadequate, as if maybe she hadn't really thought about the power of prayer. Most times, she fell asleep while praying. She and her friends prayed, but usually privately. And as far as Michael was concerned, she didn't know what to ask for. For him to come back? To send a farewell note? To let someone know if he's all right?

She'd trusted what he said to be truth. She didn't know about his secrets.

Could she trust Noah? He had secrets, too.

And then she thought about Noah's strange reaction about Loretta.

Lizzie pulled into the drive below and Megan stood. She gazed at the helpless expression on Noah's face.

She didn't expect a response from Noah when she said, "I don't know what to believe about Michael and Loretta."

He stood. "Would you like to know about me…?"

She'd just told herself she did not want to relate to Noah on a personal level, so she picked up her tote and walked over to the steps. She should just keep walking.

Hearing the car door slam, she glanced down. Lizzie stood with her face tilted up toward the deck, her red hair like a signal she was ready and able to come to Megan's defense if needed.

Unfortunately, Megan didn't know what she needed. But when Noah added the words, "…and Loretta?" to his question, her red patent-leather shoe stopped before it stepped down and she looked over her shoulder at Noah.

"Now?" he added.

She stared at the steps she should descend and never see again. She needed to forget all about Michael and Noah and the past. But then, she needed to learn from it, too. And there was so much she didn't know. Feeling the tears again she put her hand on the railing but nodded, not even sure he saw.

She walked down the blurry steps, stood beside the car and talked to Lizzie in a low tone. She tried to explain to Lizzie what had happened. When she reached the Loretta part, Lizzie gasped, as surprised as Megan had been.

"Died?"

"That's what Noah said. And he asked if I wanted to know about her."

"Do you?"

Megan took a shoulder-lifting breath then exhaled heavily. "No," she said, then changed her answer. "Yes." She grimaced. "I had just decided that Michael left me and returned to Loretta. Now this." She shrugged helplessly. "I don't know if he and Loretta divorced and then she died, or if Michael lied. It gets weirder by the moment."

"But Noah seems genuine, don't you think?"

Megan nodded. "Didn't Michael?"

"I didn't get the chance to really know him. I liked him, but then he didn't relate much at all after he had the flu."

"Now I think it was more than flu. Maybe it was cold feet." Megan looked up and saw Noah on the deck at the table with his head bent and she figured he was praying. "If I walk away now, I'll never come here again."

Lizzie smiled weakly. "Your choice, hon."

The easier thing would be to run away. Like Michael had? She relented. "I'll listen to what he has to say."

"Want me to stay? Up there, or in the car?"

"Thanks, but I need to face this." And if she knew more about Loretta, she might have some idea what it was she needed to face. Maybe Michael had loved Loretta so much he couldn't face the fact that she had died.

"Okay," Lizzie said. "But I'm as near as the phone. And just a few blocks away." She perked up. "Or I can stay here, walk around and smell the flowers."

Megan swiped at her cheeks, knowing the tears threatened now because her precious friend cared so much. "Thanks. I'll be okay."

Lizzie took the makeup kit from her purse and handed it to Megan. She caught hold of her arm. "You take care now."

"I'll call when we finish here."

Lizzie didn't budge. She looked up at the deck. "Hi, Noah," she called. "Take good care of my friend."

Noah stood with his hands holding on to the banister. His voice sounded as serious as Lizzie's when he said, "I promise."

Chapter 12

A moment ago Noah had watched Megan descend the steps. When he asked if she wanted to know more about Loretta and him, she hadn't said anything, but unless he was mistaken, she'd nodded.

Something unexpected leapt inside him. She wanted to know more about him? Just as quickly, he shook aside that errant thought. She'd want to know more about Loretta so she could understand Michael.

He'd dropped to a chair and said a prayer that their relationship would not end like this. Then he'd stepped to the banister and watched her and Lizzie talk. When Lizzie had said, *Take good care of my friend,* he knew she implied, *or else.*

He'd said, *I promise.*

But how? Megan wasn't open to that. Lizzie's car disappeared around the house and Megan headed for the steps.

What happened to his good judgment? Could a woman's tears cause him to speak so impulsively and ask if she wanted to know more about him?

If he'd minded his own business, he'd simply have gotten on with his life. With work and dating. He should have let Michael and Megan work out their own problems.

But is that what a decent person does when someone, particularly a family member, a cousin who hasn't come to terms with his past, asks him to intervene?

To be honest, Noah had thought Megan a wonderful woman before he met her. Michael's describing her and showing him her picture convinced him that if anyone could bring Michael into a life of faith and love it would be Megan.

But Michael had run away.

And yes, Noah had an obligation here. He did get involved. He was becoming friends with Megan's friends. But dread swept through him at the thought of what he had to do. It might increase Megan's heartache. His own, for that matter.

Stepping onto the deck she lifted her tote and frowned. "I need to fix my face."

He opened the screen. "You know where the bathrooms are?"

She nodded. "I'll use the one next to the kitchen."

"Fine," he said. "I need to find something in a box in the basement. You might finish before I do."

She groaned. "With the damage I've done here?" Her fingers touched her face. "I doubt it."

He smiled lamely, thinking her face depicted a woman carrying a lot of emotion inside her. Being brave. She hadn't spoken of Michael even once in anger. She was hurt. He wished he could do something to *take care* of her. Instead, what he was about to do might not help, only wound her further.

She walked toward the bathroom and he went to the basement.

It would be in one of the boxes marked COLLEGE BOOKS.

The ones he'd packed while fighting his emotional battles. Instead of fighting Michael, he'd enlisted and fought in Iraq.

The chaplain had made the difference. But long before that,

from the time he was born, he supposed, his parents had made the difference. He'd always known about faith. But he'd taken it for granted until he'd faced what was called the enemy.

He'd erased the pictures from his computer. He'd erased them from his phone. He'd tried to erase them from his memory, but that had been impossible and that's why he understood Michael.

Michael's memories were multiplied tenfold. No, a hundredfold.

Noah hadn't gone to the funeral. He'd stood far away from the burial site, watching Michael and Loretta's parents being consoled. He'd left in anguish and anger. After the first tour in Iraq, he'd returned, gone alone to the gravesite and later talked with Michael. He'd forgiven his cousin because he knew God had forgiven him, who was also guilty. He'd excused his times of failing as his being young and foolish. Some of that was true. Some was refusing to think about what he knew was right or making excuses or justifying what he wanted.

He stared into the dark basement. The odor of dust clung to the damp air, reminding him of known sin that clings to one's conscience. He switched on the light and his eyes searched out the boxes. He opened one, and there it was.

The obituary.

He did not unfold it but took it with him and waited for Megan on the deck. He turned and smiled when she walked out, aware of her lovely face, soft and smooth. The only evidence of distress was the puffiness beneath her eyes.

She ducked her head and peered at him. "I feel a little better, anyway."

He wished he did. But his apprehension rose by the moment. "It may not last considering where we're going. Maybe I should get more napkins."

She forced a laugh. They both were trying to relate…without relating.

She lifted her purse. "I have tissues now."

"Shall we?" He spread his hand toward the steps and followed her down.

After he opened the passenger side of his car and she slid in, he went around and settled in the driver's seat. As he turned the key in the engine she said, "Nice car."

"Thank you." He backed up and turned to drive around the house. "A present from my earnings while serving in Iraq."

"I'm sure you deserve it." He heard sincerity in her voice.

He stopped at the street to look for traffic. "Yes and no," he said. "A person needs to get paid for his work. But being willing to fight for one's country is something beyond a paycheck."

He saw a glimmer of warmth in her dark brown eyes when she glanced at him.

"Besides." He patted the dashboard. "I need to make an impression of success when I take potential clients to lunch or meet them at a house. A nice car says that better than a van with a logo."

He felt a moment of discomfort, wondering if that sounded egocentric. But she laughed. After a moment she said, "This morning I thought I'd make a good impression by looking somewhat professional." She shook her head. "I didn't count on the tears. Maybe I should have worn sunglasses."

He hoped a joke might maintain the light mood. "Or a face mask?"

"Ach." Her head snapped toward him. "I did look pretty yucky."

"Half of that at least."

"Yes. Yucky."

He'd thought pretty, in spite of the face-washing tears. He'd wanted to reach out, touch her, make it right, *take care*.

But he had to be careful of every word and move. He'd thought about dressing down that morning, in jeans and a T-shirt, to prove he wasn't trying to impress her. Finally, he'd decided to wear casual slacks, a dress shirt with sleeves rolled up and no tie.

"Oh," Megan said as he turned and drove through the

wrought iron arch with the name of the cemetery overhead. "Grandmother is buried here."

He asked if she wanted to go to the gravesite and she said yes. He parked on the side road. She took a packet of tissues from her tote, and after he punched the remote to lock the car, they walked down along the older section of the well-kept grounds. She stopped at a huge stone marking a gravesite not yet as level as most.

Megan's lips trembled. She held her hands in front of her skirt, tilted her head and looked lovingly, but sadly, at the stone. Noah read the name of Margaret Anne Conley. She had died recently.

"I'm sorry," he said.

She nodded. "Wish I had flowers."

Beneath the name and date was John 14:2, the scripture the military chaplain had used many times. "The verse says it all."

She gave him an appreciative glance. "Yes. She's in the place Jesus prepared for her."

Noah looked out at the tombstones. Some large granite sepulchers, some a block of cement set into the ground; others had angels on them, some crosses, some very plain, others elaborate. Some indicated that people came often and placed flowers on the graves. Others had a few weeds sprouting up.

And yet, beneath the ground, they were all the same. Gone. Perhaps some graves seemed forgotten because those remaining believed the departed one was in heaven and they didn't need to visit an empty grave.

Noticing that Megan took a tissue from the packet and wiped her eyes, he asked, "What was she like?"

"That would take such a long time to answer. But thanks for asking." She exhaled a deep breath and her gaze met his as if to say this is not why he brought her here. He turned toward a newer section. "This way," he said and she followed along beside him.

The closer they came, the more aware he was of the heady

scent of flowers. He stopped on the path beside the stone on which was etched: LORETTA ROSE HAWTHORNE, *Beloved Daughter.*

Megan kept staring, as if she couldn't take it in.

He knew the feeling.

"She was only twenty-one."

Her whispered words were barely audible. Or maybe he was only hearing his thoughts. Megan's questioning gaze shifted to him and back again. "She…kept her maiden name?"

Avoiding eye contact he stared at the tombstone. The folded newspaper clipping in his pocket seemed to burn a hole in his heart. He thought the past was settled, over with, history. But he felt it. A sweep of emotion he'd felt years ago.

He did not want to unfold the clipping.

Did not want to face it.

But he'd faced it already. Although something was over, the memory, the pain could return. But he didn't have to let it linger.

"What happened?"

He handed her the article.

Flashing through his mind was the report of the automobile accident. She'd left a party. Had been drinking. Hit a tree. Broken neck. Died on impact.

Megan took a long time to read the obituary. Maybe she read it more than once. Slowly, she folded it and looked at him. "This doesn't say she's survived by a husband. By…Michael."

"No," he said, "it doesn't."

She swallowed hard, then cleared her throat. "Were they secretly married?"

"Not to my knowledge. But I was in Iraq when this happened. I found out later."

A long moment passed before she asked, "What was she like?"

That was the question he'd asked about her grandmother

and she'd avoided answering. He would like to do the same, but he'd brought her here to tell her about Loretta.

Noah thought of the clipping Megan held in her hand. A black and white picture of Loretta. But his mind saw her in living color. Like the one he'd tried to erase from his mind. He remembered her most often in her cheerleading outfit. That's how he'd first seen her. But his was not a long story. Short, like her life.

He took the clipping Megan held out. "She was the head cheerleader for our team. Had short brown hair and dark flashing eyes. Always smiling, always talking. The first time we met, to me she smelled like shampoo and chewing gum." He laughed. "I thought that strange, after all that jumping around and being at the top of a cheerleading pyramid."

Megan smiled. "She sounds beautiful."

"She was a—" words caught in his throat "—a fun-loving girl." How much should he say? He drew in a deep breath. "Loretta was my girl before she turned to Michael." He tried a laugh as if that were just a fact, but it was a poor attempt. "He and I used to compete. In everything."

"Everything?"

Feeling uncomfortable he said, "You know, sports, even making the highest grades."

"Girls?"

"That was in our young and foolish days. We were too young to be serious."

He was finding it difficult to talk about this girl who had so much energy and potential. Now there was but a headstone with a name and a date. And no flowers.

He stepped away from the grave. Megan walked beside him as they reached the walking path that led back to the car. Maybe the breeze would dry the liquid emotion in his eyes.

"I was a senior. She and Michael were sophomores. I met her first and we hit it off right away. Then Michael made sure she noticed him. Next thing you know, the two of them were an item. It was a game we played. She chose him."

"Were you heartbroken?"

Truth? "Yeah. I told Michael I was more serious about her than any girl I'd dated. He said all's fair in love and war. After graduation I chose the war."

After a long moment she said, "The date on the tombstone is about the time Michael said they divorced, and he was so heartbroken he left college and turned to all the wrong people and things. After a year he returned to college to make something of his life." She smiled wanly. "I admired him for that." Her words were filled with irony.

"Making something of one's life can be difficult even with the Lord's help. I'd say almost impossible without."

She looked at him quickly. "But—?"

She said nothing more, but when they reached the car, she leaned back against it. He wondered what she was about to say. Maybe what Michael had told him. That he wanted to turn his life around. He'd been doing that. He'd earned his college degree. He worked with the tour company. He'd attended church with Megan.

But…where was he now?

Noah leaned against the car next to Megan. Looking at the markers of finality, he thought that was likely easier to accept than losing someone who was still out there somewhere.

Take care.

How could he ease her heartache? Maybe if he could help her understand Michael better. "I had advantages that Michael didn't. My parents had a strong faith in God. It was tough on Michael when his parents split up. He was a teenager. That's when he began to work with us during the summers and competition became commonplace. He's younger, but he wanted to outwit me. He worked hard at it. That made us both excel more in whatever we did. It didn't matter to me that we competed, until—"

"Loretta," she finished for him.

A long silence. Then she spoke quietly. "So now you and Michael no longer compete." She said it as a statement, but it felt like a question. That was puzzling. Slowly it dawned on him that she might think he was competing for her affection.

At the cemetery? He almost laughed, then sobered. A cemetery could lead to serious thought and conversation. This trip had done that. He and Megan had talked about serious matters for the first time.

Did Megan think this was a game? Michael disappears and Noah appears on the scene to compete for her? Or because Michael had taken Loretta away from him, he would try and take Megan from Michael?

Did she think he'd play fast and loose with her affections?

Try to win her over?

Should he tell her he would never do that?

Never?

Could he tell Megan he was not interested in her?

Lie?

To show interest in Megan could destroy Michael's fragile faith in him and in God.

Not to show interest would eliminate him from any possibility with this woman who already... *No, just pray, Noah.*

He could be honest enough to say, "No, I don't compete now. I try to live the way the Lord directs in my life, and it's not a game."

He reminded himself anew that if Michael took his advice, he would surrender to the Lord, put the past behind him and deserve a wonderful woman like Megan. This was not just between him and Megan and Michael. God was in on it.

She stepped over, stood in front of him and touched his arm. "I'm sorry," she said. "You must have—"

He felt the vibration of his phone. He reached back and took it from his pocket.

Megan stepped aside.

"Lizzie," he said. "She's right here." He thrust the phone toward Megan.

She took the phone and spoke into it. "I'm fine. We're at the cemetery. I left my phone in the car. Yes, I'll have Noah drop me off at Aunt B's. Be there in a few minutes." After listening for a while, she said, "I'll tell him. Bye."

She lifted her eyebrows, closed the phone and handed it to him. "They want me back. I feel an Aunt B lecture coming on."

"You mind that?"

"I love it." She smiled. "Aunt B has a way of putting things into perspective."

"You're surrounded by wonderful friends."

"I know," she said.

On the way to drop her off at Miss B's and seeing that the cemetery visit had not brought her to tears, he ventured to say, "Could we try again with our…business about my furniture?"

She glanced at him. "You have more cloth napkins?"

He grinned. "And a tablecloth."

They both were trying to keep the mood light, but she seemed tense when she got out of the car at Miss B's. He saw the trucks at the cottage and men working. He'd like to check on the progress but had a couple of other appointments. He backed up in the cottage driveway to turn the car. Megan stood on Miss B's porch. She fanned her face, making him wonder if her tears had started again.

He wondered what Miss B's perspective would be on Megan's having cried all morning.

SweetiePie and Mudd stood near the edge of the lawn at the driveway, watching him as if wondering what he was doing there.

"Frankly," he said aloud, feeling his brow furrow. "I don't really know."

Chapter 13

Noah awoke to a light breeze on his face from an open upstairs window, the morning sun beginning to rim the horizon and Megan on his mind. She'd been the last thing on his mind before going to sleep and now he prayed for her again.

He had a cup of coffee while dressing and hurried out to the fitness center to meet up with Symon and Paul. After the swim he returned to his house for Bible reading and a quick breakfast. He needed to do a lot of work at the office.

He was deep into the work when about midmorning the call came through.

"Corabeth Yarwood on line one," Miss Jane said.

Miss B? He felt like a kid in a classroom again. But he'd never had to fear her. He just didn't want to displease her. Or Megan. Or her friends. But if he had, he thought how great it would be to just get a rap on the knuckles with a ruler and be done with it.

Not so with adults. You had to endure disappointment. Theirs and your own.

"Miss B?"

"Good morning, Noah." She sounded proper. And pleasant. "Are you stopping by the cottage this morning?"

He'd done that most days. That is, when he wasn't having breakfast with Megan and taking her to the cemetery. "That's on my schedule."

"You might stop in and talk with us for a while, if you have time."

"I'll make time."

"Thank you, Noah. I'll look forward to seeing you."

"Yes, ma'am. Thank you for calling."

He hung up and then breathed. He didn't think it was work on her house she was calling about. Likely, Symon would have done that if needed. He wouldn't be surprised if she demanded he tell what he knew about Michael or that he just let Megan be.

He wanted her respect now even more than when he was a child in school. And he wanted to be real friends with Symon and Paul. If he could come out with explanations about Michael, everything would be easier. But becoming friends by abandoning Michael wouldn't be right.

A scoff escaped his throat at that. It was Michael who had done the abandoning. Noah didn't know where he was or what he was doing. He'd just have to pray, and muddle through, wondering how God was going to work all this out for good.

He took the company van and lectured himself to pray, let go and stop worrying because that wouldn't solve anything. He'd best turn on some music and sing along. So he did. And looking out along the squares and lovely historic residences, he felt the joy of his blessings. He had so much to be thankful for.

He was still counting his blessings when he turned into the drive at Miss B's. As he neared the cottage he saw Megan's car.

He exited the van and looked around but saw no one, although he heard the familiar, welcome sound of hammering. Walking around to the other side of the cottage and seeing the progress, he felt even better. The frame revealed how far into the trees the cottage would extend. It would blend in well with the landscape and make for pleasant rooms closer to the creek.

The screen door opened and Symon walked out. "What do you think?" he said with a nod toward the sound of busy workers talking, laughing and hammering while SweetiePie and Mudd played in the creek.

Noah lifted his brows. "More important is what you think."

"Annabelle," he said and grinned, "is pleased with how it's looking."

"Good," Noah said. "And I'm pleased with the progress they're making. Coming along fast, but they know we never put speed over quality." He paused. "Miss B wants to see me."

"I know." Symon turned serious and tucked his thumbs into the pockets of his jeans. "Annabelle called me and said the same. I thought it was probably to discuss…" He lifted his gaze toward the sky and back again. "…more wedding plans."

Noah shook his head. "I may be in hot water. Megan cried at my house yesterday. Then I took her to the cemetery. I may not be in Miss B's good graces."

"Only one way to find out."

Noah had no choice but to go along with Symon. They walked up the path and through Miss B's beautifully land-scaped yard. Everything was pristine, lush and green beneath moss-laden oaks and tall fragrant magnolias.

They walked across her patio. Symon knocked on the screen and called, "Coming in." Then he looked at Noah. "Never know if somebody might be in a wedding dress. Seeing that before the wedding would be a disaster. Frankly," he lowered his voice and paused a moment, "I doubt that I'll notice any-thing but that beautiful woman becoming my wife."

An instant of envy swept over Noah. A longing for someone special for himself. Why such a thought entered his mind, he didn't know. Well, yes, he did. He was a human being with all the instincts, hopes and feelings of any other human.

He focused on the positive. He was pleased that Symon offered his friendship. But he wondered how things would go after this meeting.

He wondered if he would have had the chance to be Symon's friend if Megan had not been friends with Annabelle. Symon had asked for his card at the book signing, so they might have related on a business level.

If Michael had stayed here and with the company, he could have been the one supervising or working on the cottage—and relating to Megan.

But Megan and Michael were not together, and it seemed Noah was here to help them get back together. So far, he wasn't doing too well.

They stopped at an interior door, where Symon called, "Still coming."

"It's okay," Annabelle answered, and they went inside and entered the kitchen.

Megan, Lizzie, Annabelle and Miss B looked up and stared at Noah. Miss B, in her welcoming way, said, "I'm glad you're here, Noah. We've been talking about you."

"Yeah," Lizzie said accusingly. "I heard you started a flood."

Seeing the amusement on the faces of everyone but Megan, Noah chanced saying, "No. I don't start floods. I build arks."

They reacted appreciatively, as if he'd said something clever.

"Maybe your dad named you Noah because he's a builder and wanted you to become one," Miss B said. She was a lovely woman, even in her sixties. Refined, yet pleasant.

"They have said that. Since Dad and his dad are builders, they like to tell others that's why they named me Noah." He laughed lightly. "I don't know why Dad was named Clarence."

Symon pulled out a chair from the table that sat near the windows with a view of the patio. He motioned for Noah to sit, then took a chair next to Annabelle. When those two looked at each other, Noah felt that longing he'd felt a short while before.

That changed quickly when he sat and Miss B said, "Megan told us about the waterworks."

Megan blinked and Lizzie ordered, "Don't do it, Megan. Remember, yesterday you looked like SweetiePie on her bad hair days."

Noah didn't know what to say, but coming from his mouth were the words, "I don't have another napkin on me."

Megan looked across at him and quipped, "I plan to replace that one with a box of tissues."

Ah. Did that mean she considered coming to his house again, even though her floodgates might open? The possibility touched his heart. He didn't like to think the relationship was over before it even started.

He looked around quickly. Relationship?

There wasn't one.

Not personal, that is.

Couldn't be.

Miss B said in her authoritative way, as if there was no room for rebuttal, "We have a few more invitations to hand address, then we'll have coffee and discuss those waterworks."

Before any more could be said, Willamina appeared in the doorway with her hands on her hips and spoke as sassily as she looked. "How you people expect me to fix your lunch with you sitting around in my kitchen?"

"Oops." Miss B stood. "We'll just gather these things and move to the dining room."

The women put their materials in boxes. With arms loaded, they left the kitchen. As Noah followed along behind Symon, Willamina stood inside the kitchen and stopped him. "And you, Mr. Noah. I have a bone to pick with you."

Staring into dark, wide eyes that meant business, he said, "Yes, ma'am." He'd heard the pen is mightier than the sword. He feared words might be more powerful than bullets. Even the cook was going to put in what he suspected would be more than her two cents' worth.

Maybe these relationships he desired with this group had ended before they started.

Chapter 14

Megan and the others took their stacks of envelopes into the dining room. Annabelle laid sheets of stamps on the table. "We don't want to exclude you fellows." She smiled in her beautiful way. "There are only about a hundred of these."

Symon lifted his chin and sniffed the aroma when Willamina brought a pot of freshly made coffee and set it on the sideboard. Aunt B gave a warning. "Wedding invitations and coffee are not a good combination on the dining room table." He sat beside Annabelle and reached for the stamps.

"Just be sure they're not crooked or upside down," Annabelle said, looking at Symon and then at Noah. Symon smirked and thrust his stamps toward her. She hit his arm and then they grinned at each other.

Megan loved their playful way. She thought of Michael. He'd had an outgoing way about him that attracted others. At least he did before he had the flu that seemed to have taken his energy. She couldn't blame him for that.

She'd detected a bit of humor about Noah as he and Symon

lifted their eyebrows and moved farther down the table to apply stamps to addressed envelopes as they were finished. Noah seemed serious, applying stamps to the corners of the envelopes carefully and deliberately. The fingernails on his strong-looking hands were well-groomed. She supposed he supervised more than he wielded a hammer. If he gave a report to Michael on how she was doing, he'd probably say, after all her tears, he might need to build that ark he'd mentioned to Lizzie.

But the tears hadn't been about Michael. At least, not all of them. And that's what Aunt B wanted to talk to them about. But for now, the conversation was about the wedding plans.

The outdoor wedding would take place on Miss B's beautiful front lawn and the reception would be out back.

"It's going to be a simple service," Annabelle said. "People see me when I speak at churches or model and crowds go to Symon's book signings. We want it to be more private than that."

Symon explained further. "One of our songs will be 'The Love of God,' a hymn that says His love is far greater than tongue or pen can ever tell. The tongue refers to Annabelle's speaking engagements and my writing novels."

He glanced at each of his friends. "Thanks to everyone here," he said, "I realize the importance of allowing God to be first in our lives. We want to acknowledge that we are bonded, and led, by more than human love."

Then Symon addressed Noah directly. "I have not made a lot of friends here and only a few are coming from New York and other places. Noah, of course, you're invited."

"And bring a friend or two if you'd like," Annabelle added.

"Like you, Symon," Noah said, "I've been away from Savannah for a while. I'd like to invite just my parents, if that's all right."

"Give me the address," Miss B said and wrote as he stated it.

When they finished with the stamps and Annabelle laid the envelopes aside, they fixed their coffee. Megan could tell Noah had been pleased by the invitation. But now he was being as careful as she about where to sit. Symon and Anna-belle settled across from each other and near Aunt B, who was at the head of the table. When Noah pulled out a chair next to Symon, Megan took a seat on the opposite side, leaving the place across from Noah for Lizzie.

Willamina headed for the kitchen and stopped in the door-way, hands on hips. "Don't worry about not talking loud enough while I'm fixing lunch. I've got plenty of glasses in here I can put against the wall."

"Now, Willamina," Miss B said lightheartedly. "We know good and well you'll tell us to speak up if you can't hear us."

"That I will," she said in her sassy way and disappeared into the kitchen.

Noah didn't lift his cup to his mouth but focused on Aunt B.

"First," Aunt B said, "Noah, I want to thank you for serv-ing in the military."

His face deepened with color. "My reasons for going weren't entirely noble."

"But you went. And you stayed. And I'm sure you endured much that you prefer to forget or don't want to talk about."

"Yes, ma'am." He stared into his cup.

"You must be glad that time has ended."

He quickly glanced to her face. His barely perceptible nod indicated he knew Aunt B was not making idle chat or any expected patriotic compliment about his service. All the oth-ers at the table had come to know Aunt B as a friend, a mom and a psychiatrist. Now she was a teacher in her dining room and including Noah.

He seemed to know where she was headed. With a slow blink he said, "It never really ends."

Her smile invited him to continue.

"I've been on the front lines and have seen all the atroci-ties you can imagine and more. It will always bother me." The moment of pain on his face softened. "So will the loss of my grandfather when I was eight. He was the most important person in my life at that time."

"And you still miss him."

"With pain and pleasure. When I was young, I missed the fishing trips, his teaching me to play football. But I'll always have that in my memory. Now, I miss his wisdom."

"You seem to have your life in perspective."

He shook his head. "I'm working on it."

"Well," she said, "that is a lifelong journey."

He grinned and nodded. "It's like the chaplain explained. In life we're faced with combat every day. It may be as minor as getting up and going to a job one doesn't like. It may be facing—" His words stopped at that moment, knowing what Aunt B was getting at. He took a deep breath, then continued. "Facing loss." His words became more confident. "That's why the scripture tells us to put on the armor of God every day. We're in a war. We never know when that grenade might be thrown."

Aunt B nodded. "Or be overwhelmed by the memory of one thrown in the past."

They were conversing on equal ground. Noah nodded then. "Whether on the military battlefield or right here at home."

"That's what I wanted us to talk about today. Life's grenades." She smiled, pleased. "I'd never thought of that description, but I like it."

Symon said, "I'll probably put it in a book."

Noah smiled. "Better give me credit, or I'll sue."

Megan felt the tension dissolve. She had the most wonderful friends. The discussions often were like having a Bible study or a counseling session. Topped off with some friendly banter. Noah was fitting in.

Aunt B was saying, "Sharing our feelings, admitting our grief and crying with friends is such a comfort."

"Like debriefing," Noah said. "Some kind of closure. I'm sorry I can't give Megan that, about Michael."

"No," Aunt B replied with a direct look at him. "What I wanted to explain to you both, so each of you will stop blaming yourself for what was inevitable, is that one cannot expect closure on a loss. Like you said, Noah. You still feel the pain and the pleasure. Megan does not need to feel embarrassed. And Noah, you don't need to feel at fault for her crying at your house."

Megan thought it was time she jumped into the conversation. "I know I will always miss my grandmother. Yesterday I had one of those unexpected waves of grief." She might as well say it. Aunt B would get around to it anyway. "And yes, it was about Michael, too. I've lost him. And I just want to know the truth."

Aunt B took it from there. "Noah, we don't expect you to divulge Michael's secrets. Or tell things only he should tell. But apparently we've had some misconceptions about him—or have been misled."

Megan knew it was her turn to talk about it or end the conversation. She chose to talk. "Michael said he'd been devastated by the breakup with Loretta, the divorce and trying to get his life back on track. I didn't push him for information and he didn't divulge any more. He never said she had died." She gazed at Noah. "I understand if it was too painful to talk about. He wasn't obligated to share his personal life if he didn't want to or wasn't ready." Megan turned to Aunt B. "She's taught us that."

"That's true." Aunt B looked around the table with her kind eyes. "These girls know my story and I'd like to share it with you, Noah."

Megan knew the others felt as she did. This wonderful woman they'd thought had never experienced anything but the good life had divulged her secrets. Now she told Noah about having a baby when she was sixteen, in Paris, and her parents making her give it up.

"For decades," she said, the memory a pain in her voice,

"I couldn't share my secret with anyone other than my friend Clovis. And not even with her until after she shared her trials with me." Aunt B sighed and the loving expression touched her face. "Sometimes we put our best foot forward instead of letting those close to us see our scars."

"Fortunately I don't have any problems," Lizzie quipped just at the right time to ease the tension. Their heads turned and she laughed, but it caught in her throat and her eyes teared.

Aunt B's kind gaze shifted to her. "Oh, honey, your way of covering is with your humor. All of us know that—except Noah, I guess." Her focus turned to him. "This girl is one of the bravest I know. Her parents were in a boating accident several years ago. She and Paul have had a rough time. It's done a world of good for these three girls to have lived together during their college years."

Lizzie straightened. "Aunt B is a lifesaver. But about my faults." Her green eyes flashed with pseudo-resentment. "All I have are faults. I can't even find a man who likes me for more than one or two dates."

Aunt B patted her hand. "Your day will come."

"Yeah," she said, "you'll still be saying that when I'm ninety-two."

Aunt B reared back. "I hope."

They all laughed. Megan shared a glance and smile with her red-headed friend. They had a glimpse into each other's hearts, hearts that had been broken. They related particularly well because of their scars. Annabelle's loss of her parents in the auto accident. Lizzie's in the boating accident. Megan's mom had a two-year bout with cancer, then her grandmother had died not long ago.

"I've learned the hard way," Noah said. "It's the Lord's presence with us during our trials that make us strong and able to reach out to others."

Megan looked directly at him then. "Since you're intent on helping Michael, maybe you can share with him that we all have problems. I hope we didn't give the impression we couldn't identify with his losses."

Noah's breath was audible. He looked emotional. "Your talking with me so openly means the world to me," he said. "You see, I lost someone I cared for deeply. And I lost Michael, too. Now I'm trying to get him back. He needs to understand and accept what you've talked about today."

Megan wondered who he had lost that he cared for deeply. She didn't think he meant his grandfather.

He'd lost…Loretta?

She shuddered to think how devastating it would be for her if she lost Annabelle, Lizzie or Aunt B. Glancing around, she thought of Symon, too, a more recent friend. Lizzie's brother she took for granted. And then she thought of Michael.

Had she lost Michael?

How can you lose what you never really had? But she'd thought they were growing closer. Thought they were examining their feelings and intentions. She felt sure they had been. Michael apparently came to his conclusions and…skipped town.

She just needed to know what she was dealing with.

"Yes," Aunt B said, "but we also need to remember that we're not required to tell anyone about our personal lives. We're entitled to our mistakes, our forgiveness and our choice of what and when and to whom we reveal our secrets."

"Hold on."

They all turned their faces toward the figure in the kitchen doorway with her hands on her hips. "Can we have an intermission here? Unless you're wanting to eat a burned or a cold lunch?"

"That would be a first," Aunt B said. They all laughed at her raised eyebrows. "I do believe lunch is about to be served. This conversation is to be continued."

Noah's eyes went to Megan, as if concerned about what conversation might continue. She thought of the numerous times when talk became serious or personal. Michael would say he wasn't feeling well and they would leave. Now she wondered if some of that was stress because he feared he might be encouraged to be open like her friends.

She watched as Noah ran his fingers through his beautiful hair, mussing it in that appealing way she liked about Michael. The way she had mussed Michael's hair. She'd loved the look and feel of it. Her gaze lingered.

She did not feel pain.

Maybe this was one of those pleasant times of her missing Michael.

Chapter 15

"Mr. Noah" were the first words he heard other than, "amen," after Symon said the prayer for lunch at Miss B's request. Then they all went to the sideboard.

Willamina drew his attention away from the browned crust that had already permeated the room with a warm bread aroma.

"They know already," Willamina said. "But in case you're wondering, everything in that potpie and them salad makings are from local gardens."

Seeing the pieces of white meat on the plates of the women, who were filling their plates first, he decided to quip, "Garden-grown chicken or is that turkey?"

She gave him a withering look, making him afraid she might not let him eat. Then she came close. "Don't you go sassing me," she warned. "If I didn't have ulterior motives, I'd take that plate right out of your hands."

He didn't doubt it. He smiled congenially, in spite of the warning in her dark eyes. And what did she mean by ulterior motives? Already she'd said she had a bone to pick with him.

Maybe she still intended to let him know what she thought of Megan having cried at his house, thinking he caused it. He got a distinct feeling that Willamina was as much a part of this family as these friends.

No one seemed to think the conversation strange. They might as well be talking about the warm, humid, sunny day.

At his turn, he dipped into the creamy sauce that emitted a luscious aroma and came out with a spoonful of chicken, celery, peas and carrots with a crust so flaky he thought it might melt before reaching his mouth.

"And that's sweet tea," Willamina said. "I guess you like sweet tea?"

"Yes, ma'am," Noah said. He would have said it even if he had to lie at this point. Couldn't chance losing that potpie.

He didn't want to chance losing these new friends. And yet, when they'd finished eating and Willamina began to take the plates, conversation ultimately left the food and general topics. It turned again to more serious matters.

"The grave of the young woman named Loretta is the same one Michael said he married—is that correct?" Miss B asked.

"Yes, ma'am," he said.

Aunt B nodded. "Then Michael wasn't truthful with us. I know you're keeping his confidence, so you don't need to think I'm trying to get you to betray that. What I want to do is help you understand about closure."

He had the feeling Miss B was talking about him. Megan probably told her that he'd said Loretta was his girl before she was Michael's. She might think he was grieving. In a way, he supposed he always would. How does one find closure to some things?

As if reading his mind, Miss B said, "I don't think there is such a thing as closure. There is only acceptance. And that doesn't come easily. And even with acceptance, memory of loss or hurt can well up in us, sweep through us like a floodgate being opened, and for a while it's uncontrollable. But then the Lord comes in and cleans it up, rebuilds, like you do those houses."

Noah was grateful Willamina had removed the plates and was bringing cups of coffee to the table as they continued the conversation. He hoped he concealed his surprise that Miss B was so open about her personal life.

"I accepted giving up my son," she said. "But even now, after more than forty-five years, the feeling can still sweep over me and cause an emotional reaction. Sometimes I cry. Sometimes I feel guilt. Sometimes I resent my parents for insisting I give him up. I felt they chose public opinion over their own grandson."

She shook her head. "I have to let it go all over again. Those are sweeps of emotion. And I dare say…" The look on her face was pure compassion. "Megan, you accept the death of your grandmother, but forty or fifty years from now the memory and the loss may sweep over you and you may react in an unexpected way. That doesn't mean you haven't let go. But it's a process. Your crying yesterday is a very early stage of letting go."

Megan nodded. "I don't know what to let go of concerning Michael."

"As I see it," Miss B said, "we can't help him unless he allows it. And it seems that might only happen through Noah's intervention." She turned to him again.

Noah spoke up. "I don't even understand completely what's going on with Michael. He hasn't contacted me since the morning he said he was leaving."

Aunt B nodded. "All we can do is pray."

Megan muttered. "That's what Noah says. But what do we pray for?"

"For honesty," Aunt B said. "Oh, I don't mean we have to reveal all our secrets. But if I hadn't been honest with Symon about my past and the son I gave up, we couldn't have been honest about our feelings for each other. We've always been like mother and son, although I lived here and he lived in that cottage."

She laid her hand on Symon's. "And without that honesty, Symon wouldn't have gone to Paris to find that son for me. And now," she said, placing her hand over her heart, "Dr. Beauvais, who adopted my son, is coming to visit. He will be here in time for Symon and Annabelle's wedding."

Noah felt the elation the others seemed to be experiencing. "Your son, too?"

Aunt B shook her head. "No. Toby died when he was eleven. Dr. Beauvais is bringing photographs and his memories."

Symon spoke up. "He's offered his villa in Paris for our honeymoon." A look of doubt crossed his face. "I've offered him the cottage while he's here. But I don't think the renovations will be finished in time for that. We may have to stop work for a while." He looked at Noah for confirmation.

Noah was thoughtful. "But you wanted it finished by the time you return from your honeymoon, didn't you? If the work stops for a while, then the workers will be mainly on the kitchen renovation when you return from Paris."

"Annabelle and Symon know they can stay here if they want." Miss B spread her hand, indicating the whole house.

Noah had an idea. But he didn't know how much he should take for granted with their offering of friendship. "There's another possibility," he said tentatively. "Dr. Beauvais could stay at my house and the work can continue at the cottage."

They all stared at him.

Finally Annabelle spoke. "That might be a good idea. If Dr. Beauvais is in that cottage, and Aunt B is here, who's to keep an eye on them?" Her beautiful blue eyes widened, but a grin played about her lips. "I mean, she watches my and Symon's every move like a hawk."

"No such thing," Aunt B denied, then conceded. "Well, maybe, so don't go getting any ideas." She grinned, then spoke seriously. "But I don't need watching, believe me. I had that bout of pseudo-romance and marriage for a few years when I was in my forties. That's enough for me. Besides, this Dr. Beauvais was in his early twenties when he and his wife adopted Toby. So he'd be in his late sixties. Probably old and decrepit. Too old to cut the mustard, as the saying goes."

"I met him, you know," Symon said, casting her a sly glance. "And…well, you can judge for yourself when he gets here. But considering that Megan and Lizzie work evenings, I think it might be a good idea for Noah to keep a close eye on you two."

"Oh, you," Aunt B scoffed.

Megan had another idea. "Lizzie and I could move in here with you, Aunt B. Dr. Beauvais could say in my house."

Aunt B nodded. "If you're going to turn the house into a B and B, then that's what you two girls would do anyway. But it's a lot of moving around while we've got this wedding to get under way.'

"I mean it," Noah said. "I would love to have his company. He might like to have mine. I'm gone most days. If he's a loner, that's fine. If not, I can get reacquainted with Savannah while he's getting acquainted." He laughed, then said, "I hope he cooks."

A sound came from the doorway and Willamina stood there, hands on hips. "What do you think I'm doing in this kitchen?"

"Exactly," Aunt B said. "You and he could have dinner here, or Willamina knows how to get to your house."

After a firm nod, Willamina turned back to the kitchen.

Noah's momentarily deflated mood turned to confidence that his offer might have been accepted. "All I need now," he said, "is my furniture moved out of the middle of the room."

Words sounded from the kitchen, "My daughter Doris has a cleaning service."

Seeing the grins around the table, Noah nodded. "I guess that's settled."

"I'll be glad to help move the furniture," Symon offered.

Lizzie perked up. "Why don't we all go?"

Aunt B nodded. "Megan can suggest the arrangement and I can always stand around supervising."

"Sounds like a plan," Symon said.

Willamina came in. "Is this the time to call Doris?"

Noah nodded. "As soon as possible would be good. The whole house could use a good cleaning, especially if I'm going to have company."

Everyone's smiling faces indicated Dr. Beauvais would stay with Noah.

"I might as well go, too," Willamina said. "Since you're going to hire my daughter and be lucky enough to get me as your cook. Part-time, of course. I can't cook for everybody."

Annabelle huffed. "Sure you'd have time? You're going to be working for me and Symon, too."

"Honey, I've been practicing all my life. Been working for B here since before you gals were born. Then it dwindled down to part-time. And to think, after Symon came back, everything has changed. Now me and my family are rolling in dough. Biscuit dough, that is."

Noah heard the soft chuckles. "Is that the bone you had to pick with me?"

"It ain't no funny bone."

He shook his head. "After that potpie, I'll say it's a wishbone."

"I don't work cheap."

He grimaced, beginning to see why she was one of the family. "Good thing," he jested, "I don't eat much."

Looking around, he saw that the others were chuckling and taking it in like friends do. Except one, who still held a modicum of reserve around him. She focused on Lizzie instead of on him.

He wondered… Just what could he do about that?

Chapter 16

They all went in the back way. Megan did not feel like crying. She didn't know if that was because her friends were with her and she felt supported, or if her crying had been that sense of grief and loss that Aunt B said can just sweep over a person without warning.

Regardless, she didn't feel it now.

She was, of course, aware of Michael's absence when there or any place they'd been together. If only she knew whether to feel compassion about his leaving or gratitude and anger that he had left, she'd be better able to deal with this.

But she was dealing just fine and proved it when they went into the living room and Noah waved his hands at the jumble of furniture.

Aunt B touched a couch and commented on its fine texture and colors. Everyone looked at Megan as if she had the answer to making this look like a livable room.

She felt as helpless as they looked. "I'm no expert," she said.

"Okay, let's leave," Lizzie said and turned as if she was going to walk out.

Noah plopped down on a couch and propped his legs on the nearby chair arm. "I'll just learn to live like this."

Trying to join in their playful antics, Megan touched a finger to the side of her face. "Wait. Something's coming to me."

Noah's friendly smile and the way his eyes had of narrowing in that pleased way was disconcerting. She should not give the impression all was well between her and Noah. Actually, there *was* something between them…and that was Michael.

Turning her attention to the nearest chair she placed her hand on the back of it. "Design shouldn't just please the designer. It should please the individual. What kind of living room do you want? Do you want the historic significance to be the outstanding feature?"

Perhaps her attempt at a more professional approach had worked. She saw interest in his eyes.

"For example," she continued, "my living room is conducive to a B and B. Three of us lived with grandmother, so the living room has two couches facing each other with the fireplace adjacent to them. The coffee table serves both couches. That way several people can be comfortable and relate to each other easily. Do you want—"

Noah put his feet on the floor again and he looked around. "I get what you mean. I would like the living room to be comfortable and inviting to guests. But I don't want it to look like a museum. Some of these pieces belonged to my grandparents and I don't think they got them new."

"No, these are definitely period pieces," Megan said appreciatively. She nodded to a piece that was undoubtedly a priceless antique. "That dresser will likely bear the carved initials of the one who built it by hand."

Megan looked at Aunt B, who took that as a signal to walk over and join the conversation. Being a connoisseur of her own antiques, she would recognize the value in the room. She had, in fact, offered much instruction on various pieces when Megan became friends with Annabelle and had commented on her furnishings.

Aunt B said, "Megan is right, Noah. And you're probably aware of the historic significance."

He smiled. "Dad in particular has threatened to disown me if I would even think of dispensing with any of this."

Aunt B nodded. "Would you want the house to be part of a historic tour?"

"I wouldn't mind that," he said. "People come here to see how others lived and I really like the historic pieces better than any contemporary ones I've seen." He lifted his hands and eyebrows. "I mean, I am in the renovation business, restoring homes to their former glory. But," he said, returning his attention to Megan, "I also want a livable place. One that's comfortable for a few people."

Symon grinned at him. "Sounds like you have something serious in mind."

"I hope," Noah said with a glance his way. "I don't want it to look completely like an exhibit—or like a bachelor pad."

"I know the feeling," Lizzie piped up. "I've hoped for years but nothing's happened yet, so you'd better just arrange this house to suit you and not wait around with hopes that can easily be dashed."

Megan watched as the two eyed each other, as if both knew about dashed hopes. Or were they wondering if their hopes might be met in each other? The possibilities seemed to hang in the air until Noah turned toward a chest of drawers and began discussing it. "This belonged to my grandmother. It was passed down from her grandmother and I don't know who before that. But my dad has descriptions and information about some of the pieces."

Megan heard him but at the same time she focused on Lizzie, who turned toward her, lifted her green eyes to the high ceiling and back again and shrugged as if to say there was no hope there. She supposed nothing had clicked between Lizzie and Noah.

Noah's words, "I hope," registered with Megan again. What did he hope for? Someone like Loretta?

She hadn't really thought of him as separate from Michael. Michael's cousin. Michael's confidant. Living in Michael's home. But…maybe Noah was involved with someone he hoped would live with him here.

In a way, that was like picturing Michael with someone else. This was not easy. But okay. Noah wanted a home that had historical significance and beauty, like other historic homes in the area. She liked that.

He also wanted something that would appeal to…a woman? Then, if he had a woman, why not ask her what she wanted?

But she mustn't be so personal. The others were looking at pieces, discussing, appraising, approving. The important thing right now was making this place livable. When his personal hope was realized, then whoever fulfilled it could make her own suggestions.

For now, he'd asked for hers.

"Okay," she said finally, causing the others to quiet. "These two couches could face each other. This could be an entertainment place for a group or where tourists come to see period furniture and learn about your family's background and history."

"I don't know that it's important."

"Of course it is," she said. "Your family has a well-known business that Michael said had been in the family for generations." She hated what she had to add. "If he was telling the truth."

"It's the truth," Noah said.

Megan did not like the thought that she'd believed Michael. Could she believe Noah? Or any man? She wanted to trust.

Looking around as if thinking about the furniture, she was really thinking about Michael not wanting to work in the renovation business. He had not seemed to appreciate his family's contribution to society or the area. Noah seemed to.

"She's right," Aunt B said. "My house could easily be a showplace. After all, my dad, who was a senator, lived there. People are interested in such things. They like to make connections with people and how they lived, even if they lived poorly. But, my bedroom, sitting room and kitchen are the places where I really live."

"And the front porch," Symon added.

"Oh, yes." They exchanged an affectionate look. Thinking of Aunt B's house, the historic significance of that antebellum mansion and yet the homey coziness of most of it, Megan had an idea. "Let's go into the bedroom next to the kitchen."

They followed her.

"I'm just going to pop in to the kitchen and dining room," Willamina said.

Megan stepped into the bedroom and moved aside so the others could enter. "You really don't need a designer," she said. "The design of the house and furniture with a few additions of accessories would be perfect. I can only give my opinion of arrangement." She shrugged. "And so can everyone else."

No one else said anything, so she figured her opinion was expected first. "Okay," she began, "The first time I looked in this bedroom I thought it would be ideal as a sitting room or den. It's more private than the other rooms, having windows only on the one side." She gestured to the windows. "It's next to the kitchen and there's a fireplace where one could read, or eat or whatever. For one person—or two, in particular. It's cozier than the kitchen and more inviting than the spacious dining room."

Noah looked surprised. "I never thought of turning a bedroom into a sitting room."

"It's just a room," she countered. "It's only the bed that makes it a bedroom."

"And that could be moved out," he said reflectively.

"Exactly."

He was nodding. His hint of a smile made those appealing creases at the side of his mouth. Michael's had been more at the center of his cheeks. Dimples. Like a cute kid, at times. At first. Then it changed and Michael hadn't smiled very much.

Which had been the real Michael?

The happy-go-lucky one?

Or the morose one?

Which had been the pretender? She didn't know. She didn't really know Michael after all.

They'd talked about the house. He'd showed it to her. Had mentioned the historic significance, but he hadn't seemed to care about that. Now she wondered why Michael had brought her here in the first place. Then, she'd thought it was because of her interest in anything historical. Now she wondered if it had been a ploy to get her alone.

He had seemed more ardent here. But she hadn't thought that unusual, their being alone in his house. Now, she'd lost perspective or trust in many things and people. Michael hadn't been interested in the house as much as he'd been interested in her. She'd felt complimented. Now she wondered. About him. About his motives. Had he really been serious about her in a lasting way? Or was it only temporary?

She shook away the thoughts as her friends were discussing her suggestion and seeming to like it. After a while Noah's eyes met hers. They held that silver glint. They darkened when he was concerned. They brightened when he was pleased.

"I like the idea," he said. "Very much. You're right. This is a big house with a lot of rooms. Why not have the combination of history reminding me of my ancestry and yet have my own private spots?" He turned his animated face toward Aunt B. "Like Miss B said about her house."

He turned to the others. "I'm not even sure," he said, "which was Michael's bedroom."

Megan stared at him, saw the color creep into his face as his eyes darkened and he looked away. She knew, and she didn't mind saying it. Knowing where someone's bedroom was didn't mean… She spoke clearly. "It's upstairs. The first one on the right. And the bedroom next to it would make a beautiful sitting room for a woman, in particular. She could look out on that lovely backyard, watch the morning sun come into the room. A small balcony could be built where the windows are."

"Well," Noah said, touching the wooden headboard amid a few chuckles. "Who wants to help me take that bed down and put it into the basement?"

All the women pointed to Symon, who said, "I think I might volunteer."

Willamina stuck her head into the room. "You might want to get Doris and her crew in here to clean everything, including the baseboards, before you start pushing that furniture up against the walls."

"Good idea," Noah agreed. "That reminds me. I have a crew that's expert at moving." He grinned. "And I think I can get them at a reasonable price."

They all laughed and then Noah offered a tour of the house. "Maybe you could suggest which would be the best room for Dr. Beauvais." He turned to Symon. "He's able to do stairs all right, isn't he?"

"As able as Aunt B." Symon chuckled and grinned at Aunt B, who gave him a warning look and said, "You be careful, son."

They all toured the house and the backyard, where Symon, having been the son of Aunt B's caretaker, gave some expert advice. For the most part, one couldn't improve on the natural growth of live oaks, magnolias and azaleas.

Noah looked content. When they were ready to go he thanked them profusely. "You all make me feel like I'm coming back to life. Not just with—" he looked over his shoulder "—the house." He turned to them again with that endearing look. "But in my personal life. Readjusting to everyday life isn't as easy as one might suppose."

"We need each other," Aunt B said, "but it's that faith you've talked about that will see you through difficult adjustments."

He nodded.

"Good food helps, too," Willamina said. "I left Doris's and my cards in your kitchen."

"Thanks," he said, looking pleased.

As they walked to their cars, Noah said, "Megan." She stopped.

"I still need you to tell me, and the crew, where to put the furniture." He paused. "If you will."

"I said I would." She glanced at Lizzie, who walked a few steps away and picked at an azalea leaf.

Megan glanced again at Noah and jested, "I don't have a card."

"Of course I'll pay you anyway."

Her breath caught. "I was trying to joke. There is no charge." Glancing at Lizzie she saw a lush green leaf float to the ground. Megan shook her head. "All I might do is give an opinion on arranging furniture."

"But the sitting room idea was such a perfect suggestion. It suits me and what I want in my house, but I wouldn't have thought of it. To show my appreciation," he began before she could form a coherent word, "why don't I come by your house and express my opinion about what might be changed for a B and B?" He grinned. "And I do have a card."

"Well, like you said, you do have a business and I don't expect you to make a free house call."

He was shaking his head. "Megan. I was trying to joke."

It was her turn to shake her head. She hated the idea they had to be so careful with each other. As if he was an enemy. He must think her a complete ninny.

She was about to say to forget the whole thing. Anybody

could give an opinion about where to put furniture, and if it didn't look right, you could move it.

But Lizzie walked up to them. "In the morning would be perfect, wouldn't it, Megan? Tomorrow's your day off so you don't have to think about getting ready for work. And I'm not joking."

Nevertheless, Noah chuckled. "After my morning swim, I have a project I want to check on. Could we have lunch and discuss the B and B?" He touched his forehead, where the golden platinum hair fell over his brow in that free style. "But you have brunch, right?"

"Unless I have something else planned. I can grab a cup of coffee and a bagel or something."

"Fine. It's a date." He added quickly on a thin breath, "I'll call you."

The color that rose to his face was likely the same as hers. A date?

Not a date date.

That was just another word for appointment.

Chapter 17

The next morning, Megan was still explaining the meaning of "date" to Lizzie, who continued to tease her about it. Megan picked up her ringing phone and, seeing who the caller was, turned on the bar stool away from Lizzie's inquiring green eyes.

"Hello?" She listened. "Yes, that's fine. All right. Sure. Bye." After a deep breath she turned again to her bagel and coffee.

"Was that your date calling?" Lizzie said slyly.

Megan gave her a warning look. "It's not that kind of date," she protested. "Remember, you and I are going to be single all our lives."

With the flip of her hand Lizzie slung her hair out of her face. "He called it a date."

Megan countered. "A date can also be an appointment or a meeting. That's what this is. He's nursing a broken heart and I see him as an unreasonable facsimile of Michael."

"Right. And you don't want to repeat history, do you? Like getting back with Michael?"

"I don't know how I'm to feel about Michael. I don't know him. And I don't know Noah. And don't want to. This meeting is like an interview to see what either of us thinks about this house being a B and B. I don't even know if I'd go with his company."

"Where's he taking you for lunch?"

She wiggled her ponytail and lifted her chin. "He's not. After I show him the second floor, I'll simply tell him that I don't feel like going to lunch." She huffed. "And I'm sure not fixing lunch for him here."

Lizzie looked askance. "You think he'd expect that?"

"No, not really." Megan sighed. "We're both careful about each other. Anyway, I'm not dressed to go out anywhere." She'd given thought to her clothing and was in khaki twill knee-length shorts and a sleeveless V-neck cotton jersey camisole with an empire waist. Its white background sported strawberry, black and khaki stripes. The clothing expert Annabelle had helped her pick the outfit. It was casual enough not to imply she was dressing up for him. "After we talk about the B and B, I'll just say we don't need to go to lunch and I really should go to Aunt B's and discuss wedding plans."

At Lizzie's stare and shake of her head, Megan said, "That's not lying. It's something you and I do at every opportunity." At Lizzie's grin she said, "What?"

"I don't know. For some reason I thought of Shakespeare and his *methinks* remark."

Megan gasped. "I'm not *protesting* about anything. I just don't…don't…" She had to think a moment. "Don't want to give him any more ammunition for his report to Michael."

"He can't very well report if he's not in contact with him."

A sense of helplessness lifted Megan's shoulders in a shrug. Did Noah really not know where Michael was? Was his family trying to find him? How would they know whether he's all right?

The doorbell chimed.

They both headed for the front. "Must be him," Lizzie said. "Wonder why he didn't park out back?"

"Gentlemen pick their dates up at the front door."

Megan looked out the living room window while Lizzie headed for the foyer. "I don't see his car."

"Maybe you're going to walk for lunch."

Megan nodded. "Now that's gentlemanly, isn't it?"

"Depends." Lizzie opened the door. "Hi, Noah. Come in. And thanks a lot. Because of you, I even did a little house-keeping this morning."

He laughed. "You thought that necessary, after seeing the mess I live in?"

She shook her head. "Megan made me do it."

She stretched out her hand toward the living room as if presenting Megan. He stepped in and said, "Good morning."

"Morning," she said, thinking he didn't look a mess. Well, except his silvery blond hair. It had that messy groomed look that she'd thought so adorable on Michael. Noah's seemed even fuller, as if begging for fingers to muss it or sweep it back. It looked as if the wind had whipped it to one side while locks fell over part of his forehead in a casual way to complement his attire.

His light-colored cotton pants were topped by a tucked-in black polo. Casual but very presentable. He made a good appearance. After all, he was a swimmer and a builder. He hadn't dressed up for her.

Good.

"Why don't you have a seat?" Lizzie said what Megan should have.

After all the times she'd seen him, he still made her uneasy. "Oh, sure. Or, we can go on upstairs and see what you think of the next floor."

He came further into the living room. "I thought we'd have lunch first since it's noon and you promised to eat only a bagel."

"It wasn't a promise. I—"

"I'm kidding," he said and she heard a bell clang.

The glance between Megan and Lizzie collided, but he grinned. "Sounds like our transportation has arrived."

She glanced out the window and saw the brown horse and white carriage. "What?" That was all she could manage to say.

He lifted his shoulders. "I thought you deserved more than a simple thank-you for my new den. Shall we?"

She ignored his outstretched hand. Of course he didn't expect her to take it. It was just a gesture to accompany his words. Too surprised to think of an excuse not to go, she walked toward him. Or was she pushed? She felt the tapping of Lizzie's fingers on her back and heard a soft giggle.

Holding on to the curved iron railing as she descended the steps of her Jones Street home, she was also holding her breath. Then she gasped. "Carl?"

"My lady," he said, with a twinkle in his eyes and a lift of his top hat, exposing his gray hair.

"What are you—?"

He tried to look apologetic. "Noah came in last evening talking about a private tour and I volunteered. Told him I was like a daddy to you."

"Thanks," she said and meant it. Having Carl there made her feel more at ease. She'd told him about Noah, and it turned out that Carl knew his parents and their business.

She said the obvious. "I guess I don't need to make introductions."

"Hi, Carl," Noah said, then made a slight bow and held his hand out to Megan. She took it for a moment, thinking it strong and smooth and capable, then stepped up and sat on the plush white leather seat.

Noah walked around to the other side. As he hopped up and settled beside her, Megan looked at the house again, seeing exactly what she expected. Lizzie stood at the window, her hand waving like a windshield wiper and her face wearing a toothy grin like a chimpanzee's. She shouldn't have looked.

"Gid-dy yup," Carl said, and the brown mare did.

Megan looked at Noah. "What are you doing?" She lowered her voice. "Or…why?"

He said, "I thought I owed you a pleasant time after the last excursion."

She knew he meant the time at the cemetery.

"You don't owe me anything."

"I feel that I do. Not from anything I've intended. But I remind you of Michael. I'm related to him. I spied on you. I live where he lived, even bought the house. I'm doing things to the house you would have done with Michael."

Yes, he reminded her of Michael every time they had a conversation.

"The brochures say this is a perfect way to spend time in The Garden City."

She chuckled. "I've repeated that enough times."

"You said you love the history. So I thought we'd just drive through and you could enjoy the ride without having to talk about it."

That was thoughtful of him. And rather creative. Had he been Michael, she would have thought it romantic. Yes, he reminded her of Michael.

"I've often thought I'd like to take the historical tours or just walk around—not talk at all, just absorb."

"Then do," he encouraged and leaned back in silence.

Megan thought of the squares where houses of many periods, buildings and lush landscapes blended uniquely together. She was absorbed.

As they rode along the squares she couldn't help but think of it the way she explained it to tourists. This was the core of Savannah, Georgia, a National Historic Landmark since 1966. She could almost hear the spoken words about the series of neighborhoods, each wrapped around parklike squares and connected by straight streets. The median strips resembled linear forests.

She smiled as they passed a group of schoolgirls walking within a square where live oaks were draped with their banners of Spanish moss. Patches of sunlight mingled with dark-velvet shade.

A couple of girls carrying portfolios reminded her of days when she strolled along like that, ready to make sketches for a written report on Savannah's history.

Like she'd told tourists, the squares with their benches and sculptures invite sitting and contemplating or just strolling along the brick walkways.

Although loving it, she could stay silent no longer. With a quick glimpse at Noah, who sat back as if enjoying the silence, she spoke as they neared Oglethorpe Square. "The first settlers were refugees from British debtor prisons. They were brought to above the Savannah River in 1733 to a barren, sandy bluff." She inhaled deeply. "Just look at Savannah now."

The slight turn of his lips made those appealing creases at the sides of his mouth. A gleam of silver sun and a sly look appeared in his eyes. "I might be able to tell you something you don't know."

She lifted her eyebrows as an invitation to try but was met with more silence. When they neared Chippewa Square he said, "Slow, if you will, Carl."

His arm moved to behind her and against the back of the carriage seat. He leaned toward her, not touching but making her aware of his closeness.

"My ancestor came over with Oglethorpe." His left arm extended as he pointed to the monument of James Oglethorpe. "He was one of the 113 who settled the colony that began building the community."

She heard his words and kept her face turned toward the statue, but was aware of his hand that dropped to rest on the curve of the carriage seat. He continued to speak with pride.

"Some of my ancestors went in different directions—cotton, fishing—but my immediate family have always been builders."

She was surrounded by him and inhaled a faint fragrance of something akin to spice and musk, just enough to make her inhale more deeply, wanting more of the pleasant scent. When he talked, his breath was warm and teased the side of her face.

Her heartbeat quickened. Any movement from either would make them touch. So close, and yet so far away. The sound of silence was heavy except for the slow rhythm of the wheels and the clip-clop of horse's hooves.

Slowly her head turned and his face was there, so close she couldn't really see it until he moved back at the same time he withdrew his extended left arm and lay his hand on his pants leg. He looked as surprised as she felt.

Why did she feel as if they had...touched? His shoulders rose as he turned and leaned against the back of the white leather seat. His parted lips closed and his blue eyes gazed straight ahead as if history was there instead of on the sides of the street.

She turned her face from him and stared at the squares and statues. At history. Had he been Michael and she had turned toward him, his arms would have tightened around her. His lips would have found hers. At least in the early days, when he was happy to be with her.

Slowly she looked straight ahead, but her glance slid toward the light-haired man beside her. He was not Michael. Those were not Michael's arms. Nor Michael's lips.

Michael would have held her and she would have been the one to hold the reins, to say "whoa" at the proper time.

She'd thought he had loved her.

Now she wondered.

He was gone.

And she felt bereft.

But it didn't last. It was that sweep of emotion that threatened. But it only threatened; it didn't attack. It did not cause her chest to ache, her throat to tighten or her eyes to tear.

She could not wish those were Michael's arms around her. Not for the arms of someone who abandoned her. The ache had likely been over the feeling of having been humiliated, abandoned, embarrassed.

Nothing happened here. Except she was sitting by someone who had reminded her of Michael. But he was not Michael. She took a deep breath and said cheerfully. "You probably know where Forrest Gump sat to eat his chocolates."

"That's something everyone should know." He laughed. "Speaking of food—"

She laughed then. "Yes, chocolate is definitely food."

"I have something else in mind." He called up to Carl. "Carl, I think it's our lunchtime."

"Yes, sir." Carl turned the carriage.

She figured they'd go to River Street to one of the many eating places. Instead they ended up at Paula Deen's restaurant. Noah hopped out and went into the restaurant. Carl turned and said, "I like him, Megan. He's like a grown-up version of Michael."

"Maybe too much like Michael," she said.

He gave her a fatherly look. "Does that make you like him too much? Or dislike him too much?"

She answered quickly. "I don't like him too much. And I don't dislike him. He's just Michael's cousin to me."

Carl winked, then turned around again as Noah jumped up into the carriage with a market sack. "You want to eat in the carriage or go home?"

"Home," she said.

Carl commanded, "Megan's home, dobbin."

Noah looked at her. "Have you done this before?"

She shook her head. "Have you?"

"Nope. This is a first."

One might consider that romantic. But she didn't. She knew it was just historic.

When they got back to Jones Street, she leaned forward to thank Carl. Noah came around and extended his hand to her in a gallant way. After all, that is the way it was done in historic times.

He bowed his head of sunlit hair and bent over her hand. But he didn't press his lips to it. After all, this was not historic times. Her feet were solidly on the redbrick sidewalk and in the present moment.

Her glance shifted to Carl, who led the horse away.

Chapter 18

Noah had a divided mind about how Megan would react to this business lunch. Holding the sack of food he followed her into the kitchen. She seemed at ease. "I'll get plates while you unload the food," she said. "That trip worked up an appetite. And if anybody knows how to cook, it's Paula Deen."

"Agreed." He opened the sack but stopped when she looked over her shoulder with a worried brow. She warned, "Don't dare tell Willamina I said that."

He laughed and relaxed somewhat, then felt more at ease when Lizzie walked in. "Do I smell chicken?"

"There's plenty here," he said. "Join us." As if it was his kitchen.

Megan smiled and set three plates on the table.

Lizzie took utensils from a drawer. She shook her head. "I guess I can take a break from seeing if those Christian singles groups have any new guys that look halfway decent."

"Halfway?" Noah said, putting the carton of fried green tomatoes next to the chicken.

"I'm desperate," Lizzie explained while picking up the container of sauce. She removed the top and sniffed. "Ohhh, this is that sweet onion relish with roasted red peppers. Yummy. Where are those biscuits? I reckon they're cheesy garlic."

"What else?" he said, although he hadn't known to special order them. "I opted for sweet tea."

"Perfect," Lizzie quipped. "When you're invited to lunch, you shouldn't have to make your own coffee." She gave him a superior look. "Or tea."

"You ain't seen nothing yet," he teased and pulled out the desserts, a sampling of Paula's famous "gooey gutter-cake" and pecan pie.

"But really," Lizzie said. "I'll just go back to my little corner of the bedroom while you two eat."

"No way," both Noah and Megan said at the same time.

Lizzie nodded. "I figured you were smart enough to say that."

"Pray for us?" Megan asked, which pleased him. He offered a short prayer. He was glad Lizzie joined them. She had a forthright way of putting others at ease and making them laugh.

After they made some general comments and mentioned the upcoming wedding, he felt comfortable enough to ask, "By the way, what was that private joke Symon and Annabelle have about the creek?" At Megan's grin, he said, "Or is it too private for me to know?"

"Not at all." Megan laughed and told about Annabelle and Wesley having taken for granted that they would marry. Their families expected it. Then Symon, as the caretaker's son, had returned to the cottage. He and Annabelle tried to be just friends, but one day when Symon was fixing a washed-out area on the bank of the creek, he tried to rescue his lame dog, Mudd, who had run from SweetiePie, and he fell in. Annabelle had followed SweetiePie down to the creek. When Mudd climbed out he began to shake. Annabelle tried to get away, but she slipped in the mud and fell into the creek.

Her face was animated. "He tried to catch her, and both ended up sitting in the creek. Without meaning to, they kissed." She sighed and seemed to have a look of longing. "Not once, but twice. So romantic."

He could imagine the kiss being romantic. But the creek? "Wasn't that kind of cold?"

"No." Her face was dreamy. She looked…kissable. "Love, I think," she said, "is warm."

"I've taken out a couple women since returning to the States and you're right. Being close is warm. But I don't think I'd kiss either of them in the creek."

"Then maybe that wasn't love," Lizzie said.

"No, it wasn't," he could say quickly. "It was just…relating."

Megan laughed. "That was the day Mudd and SweetiePie became friends, too. They were in the creek together. That was SweetiePie's bad hair day."

He saw her glance at his hair then look away. Was she thinking of the characteristic both Michael and he were noted for?

He shook the thought away. "Now I understand a little better why the creek is so important to Symon and Annabelle."

Megan nodded. "It's so romantic that they have such a dramatic conversation piece to relate about their being in love. They hadn't admitted it and still didn't for a while. But that kiss was the defining moment."

She shrugged, looked a little uncomfortable and turned her head. Was she thinking of a defining moment with Michael? Or would she like to have a defining moment? He supposed women thought that way. Actually, he wouldn't be disinclined to having a defining moment himself.

His thought had to stop there. He focused on the knife Lizzie was wielding to cut the desserts into small pieces so they could all have some of each.

After lunch he went upstairs with Megan.

"We haven't used the upstairs in many years." The stale air said as much. "Of course, there were exceptions. Guests.

College friends. Special groups. Things like that. Lizzie, Annabelle and I lived downstairs."

She showed him each bedroom, mentioned that one between two might be divided to make a small sitting area for each room. There might be a small balcony added to the rooms at the back of the house. Steps and an outdoor entry could be added for the upstairs rooms in case a guest came in late.

She looked at him for his comments. "It's certainly doable," he said. "None of it hurts the basic structure. Sitting rooms and a balcony will enhance. More inviting than four walls."

She smiled, seeming to like what he was saying.

"But you had said you weren't sure. Are you now?"

She hesitated. "I'm not positive. But I'm sure enough to want plans and information on what it entails, including cost."

"Of course," he said. "Um, just wondering. Would you operate the B and B? Live here?"

"I don't know. I'm not too keen on having strangers in my house, so it would mainly be for those I screen or know about. I mean, friends of ours might like something like this. Parents of friends. Aunt B knows everybody. Symon is planning conferences, and he often has businesspeople come in. After he's married, he might prefer their staying at a B and B instead of in the cottage or at Aunt B's."

He nodded, understanding.

"So," she said. "I don't know if I'd continue to live here."

As they walked back down the hallway and descended the stairs, she continued with her ideas. "Even if I don't decide on a B and B, I will probably want the changes made. It would be more appealing to friends who come to visit."

She invited him out into the pleasant backyard and gestured to a grassy spot near the house. "That might be the perfect place for an outdoor fireplace with a stone seating area. I'd like that for myself, whether or not this is a B and B."

"And the changes will increase the value considerably in case you ever want to sell."

"Not likely I would. After all," she grinned, "it has historic significance."

He stepped back, stood near a towering magnolia and studied the house, visualizing the addition of a patio, balconies and an outside entrance.

That divided mind of his was working, too. If she turned the Jones Street house into a B and B and Michael returned, is this where they would live? As far as he knew, all Michael had was a car. He couldn't have made much money as a tour guide. His mom had paid his college expenses and let him live in her house. But what did Michael have to offer a woman?

Of course he knew.

Who would want a man because he had a house, a job, a bank account? Even Lizzie, who seemed intent on finding a man, had said a few from the dating service seemed to have everything but nothing clicked between them.

No, there had to be that unexplainable factor.

Love.

And what man would want a woman whose main concern was…things?

At the same time, Megan didn't need the things any man had. She had her own. Her relationship with Michael was apparently based on love.

His attention was drawn back to her when she said, "Thank you." He felt this was dismissal time. He became aware of the fragrant magnolia, which was not nearly as tantalizing as the light scent he'd detected about her. It had been most tantalizing when he'd been close to her when telling about his ancestry. Something about it made him want to experience more.

She walked closer to him. "I enjoyed the carriage ride and lunch." She waved her hand at the house and yard. "And your letting me talk about changes in the house seems to establish that more firmly in my mind. I'm even more inclined to have the changes made. It's a big house and should be shared."

He nodded. "I'll put together plans and costs. I understand

you might want another company's opinion. That's how business is done." He wasn't sure he should speak the thought that occurred. But it came out anyway. "Business has its place. Friendship is separate."

Her gaze shifted away from him and he thought he might be assuming too much. He dared venture further. "I thought you saw me today instead of Michael."

Her face clouded. "I know you're different. But still, you're such a reminder of him." She reached up, and he thought she was about to touch his hair, maybe brush it off the side of his forehead. He felt it there, felt the light breeze teasing his forehead. Like her fingertips might feel if she did that. And what would he do? He'd try to laugh, or joke, anything but...

She shook her head as if to discount whatever she'd intended. Her hand fell and found a place in the pocket of her shorts.

He decided to try and joke around. "I'll dye my hair if that helps."

At her small laugh he had to smile. "Shave my head?"

"Would you really go that far?"

"No." All teasing aside he said, "If you can't see me as anyone other than a reminder of Michael, a change of my hair wouldn't do it." He paused. "Would it?"

"No." She looked serious, too. "I see a family resemblance with Lizzie and Paul. Mainly their red hair, although Paul's is darker. I also see them as entirely different persons."

But, he wondered, does she like what she sees?

She admitted, "You do remind me of him. I mean, there's a connection." He waited to see what her thoughtful expression was about. Then she said, "What makes you think I saw you differently today?"

He smiled. "Because you asked me to pray before lunch. I felt that meant you might have forgiven me for having invaded your privacy. That you might consider trusting me, accepting me as a friend, like your friends have." He paused. "Someone like you doesn't ask a person to pray unless you feel they have a close relationship with God."

Seeing her surprised look he added, "Even if it's about fried chicken."

Ah, she had a lovely smile. It transformed her already beautiful face. "I didn't analyze it," she said. "It just seemed like that's such a part of you. I think that openness about praying distinguishes you from Michael more than anything else."

"Maybe," he said and felt the words. "Maybe I pray a lot because I need it so much."

Like right now, standing in front of a woman any man would be proud to call his own. Any man…except Michael? Maybe her wanting Michael had something to do with wanting what you couldn't have. The forbidden fruit.

Is that what he was feeling? A longing for something, someone he couldn't have?

Megan said, "It's not just you. Right now I'm confused about Michael. About relationships. About what was real and what was imagined. I wouldn't be receptive to…any man."

"I understand. I wanted to escape situations and landed in the midst of a war." He tried to smile. "But in that war, I found what is most important. It's not just staying alive, but it's having the Lord in one's life, whether in good times or bad." How to keep one's distance and at the same time offer openness, he wasn't sure. However, he ventured to say, "If you want to know me, just ask."

She nodded. Then she gazed into his eyes, and he thought he'd better start praying before his hands or his feet moved toward her. And they were about to until she looked up at him and asked, "Were you in love with Loretta?"

He felt his chest rise. He glanced away from her, remembering the words of Miss B, who said you don't have to tell everything. And this was too serious, too personal, unless…

He brought his gaze back to her and asked, "Are you in love with Michael?"

As soon as he asked he felt he'd been too bold. But she looked thoughtful, not offended. She obviously knew what their questions meant.

They were really asking if they had any purpose in disclosing their own heartfelt secrets.

No need to answer.

They were bonded by their individual relationship with Michael.

And yet, what bonded him and Megan also separated them.

She gave a small laugh, as if reading his mind. But it wasn't his mind, really—it was the facts of life.

"I should go," he said.

"I'll walk around to the front with you. I think an outside entrance would be best at the back or other side of the house, but see what you think."

They walked along the driveway, which was bordered by lush green shrubs. When they came to the front steps the builder in him surfaced. "No, that side of the house shouldn't be changed."

"That's what I thought."

He narrowed his eyes. "You were testing me."

She didn't deny it. She lifted her hand and twirled her long ponytail. "My turn. Isn't that what you were doing with the carriage ride?"

"Exactly." And he didn't want to add the obvious. That he wanted her to see him as himself and not an unpleasant extension of the person he was tired of thinking about.

And she hadn't cried. In fact, her beautiful face was aglow with the sun on it and her smile. He reached for her hand, which he'd already noticed had slender fingers and curved nails. An artist's hands, he supposed. What was he going to do with it? She didn't pull away, and she wasn't smiling, just looking beautiful.

So he lifted her hand and bent his head to touch it with his lips. "That's the way a carriage ride should end," he said, as if he had to explain it. Then he added what Carl had said: "My lady."

With a lifted hand, he turned to go.

"Thank you," he heard as he walked briskly away. He felt good about today. She hadn't cried. In fact, they'd laughed together. She'd been accepting. He thought of SweetiePie and Mudd being supposedly natural enemies. But they had become friends.

Maybe he and Megan could be like that. They couldn't chase each other, but maybe they could manage to sit side by side and watch what was going on with their friends.

This was a beautiful, clear sunny day in Savannah and he felt sunshine in his soul.

Chapter 19

Megan stood for a moment, watching Noah stroll along the redbrick sidewalk. She thought he was singing. She'd heard him do that before.

His silvery hair reminded her of SweetiePie and how she loved to caress the feline's soft white fur.

That surprised her. Until now, she'd thought of his hair only in relation to Michael. Could she really accept him as Noah, separate from the past and her history with Michael?

He'd planted a feathery touch of his lips on the back of her hand. She could still feel it. But that was fantasy. They'd played a historical game.

Michael and Noah had played games. They'd competed. Michael had won Loretta.

And Loretta was in the graveyard.

Had Michael been playing some kind of game with her? She almost laughed at the irony of that. Whether or not it was intentional, he was playing a game with her.

The guessing game.

But for a while today she saw Noah, separate from Michael.

As she watched him disappear around the corner she realized she'd lifted her hand to her lips. The hand that his lips had touched.

See Noah as a person in his own right?

Yes, that was good and right.

But see him as anything more than a friend?

No. She'd better not. She must remember the hurt of the past, and learn from her heart and ego having been trampled, lest history be repeated. It would be a long, long time, if ever, before she was ready to consider having any man in her life.

Of course, Lizzie was waiting in the living room when Megan walked in. "Well, that was unexpected, wasn't it?"

"Yes, and get that look off your face. It was business."

"Business?" she squeaked.

"Yep. Like Symon's editor, who takes him to lunch because he wants his books. Noah treated me to lunch because he wants my business."

In a singsong tone Lizzie said, "He added a carriage ride."

Megan spoke defensively. "If you noticed, he didn't ask—he sprang it on me. He knew I'd say no. He's trying to reel me in."

At Lizzie's lifted eyebrows, Megan added, "I mean, for business purposes. My renovation will be an expensive project."

You'd think Lizzie had become Willamina, hands on hips and talking sassy. "And the hand-kissing?"

Megan gasped. "You spied on us?"

"Well, of course." She lowered her hands. "Isn't that what accountability partners are for?"

Megan rolled her eyes. "In broad daylight?"

"That's when they catch you off guard."

"You're an expert?"

"Well, I should be. I've dated two-thousand five-hundred eighty-seven guys and have another lined up for Friday night."

"It was nothing. The end of a historic tour. It's not like… it's not like…"

Lizzie was grinning. "Falling in the creek?"

"Hardly."

Lizzie laughed. "I'll bet if it had been your lips instead of your hand, he would have melted you like butter on a hot biscuit."

Megan shook her head to try to rid herself of not only Lizzie's quip but also the idea of Noah's lips, which were really quite appealing. Such an idea was out of the question. "You're impossible." She marched out of the room, still hearing Lizzie's soft laughter as if she'd read her mind.

It was Lizzie who had unfulfilled romantic ideas. Not her.

And she proved it by getting on with more than thinking about a man. All the thinking in the world didn't change the fact that Michael was history.

Each morning for the next week, whenever Megan and her friends had time, they went to Noah's. Megan directed the arranging of furniture, and everyone helped move it into place after Doris and her crew had done a thorough cleaning.

"Land's sake," Willamina screeched. "You call this empty room a pantry?" She huffed. "Looks more like Old Mother Hubbard's cupboard to me."

She slammed the door and placed her hands on her hips. "Nobody can cook with nothing to cook with, sonny."

"Get what you need. Change the kitchen. I'm inept in a kitchen," Noah admitted.

"That you are." Shaking her head, she marched to the cabinets and began to take out the dishes, separating good china from everyday. She looked over her shoulder at them all and shooed them away. "Go take care of your business. Kitchen's mine."

Megan took hold of Noah's sleeve and jerked her head toward the hallway. Laughing, they left.

By Friday afternoon Noah's kitchen was stocked, the house was clean, furniture was in place and the bedrooms were ar-

ranged in a way that would entice any guest. The living room
was a showplace of period furniture of historic significance, a
room where one might sit and discuss the conversation pieces
yet feel welcomed into another era.

Megan was pleased that the room Noah liked best was the
bedroom they'd turned into a comfortable cozy den. "It's my
day off," she said. "Let's shop for a couple lamps. And you
need pictures."

"I brought some paintings from my parents' house that belonged to my grandparents. We'll look those over and see what
you think. Some are originals."

"I'll take your word for it," she said, smiling. "I'm not an
art expert."

A silver glint touched his eyes. "You're on your way."

She started to negate that, then realized how many times she
refuted compliments. So she nodded instead. "I do think my
sketches of SweetiePie's bad hair days are unique and original."

Her eyes went immediately to his hair that was not like Michael's, not like SweetiePie's, but like Noah's. Thankful for his
soft laugh, she focused again on the paintings.

They shopped for just the right lamp that would be ideal
for reading while relaxing in the big overstuffed chair with
feet propped on the ottoman. After they returned, that's what
Noah did.

Megan was delighted that he loved the room, as she did.
She sat on a couch near his chair. "This is perfect for someone
just to relax and think or whatever."

"I like it," she said.

"Let's break it in."

"Break—?" her eyes questioned.

He nodded. "I can whip up a mean tomato sandwich, or banana if you prefer, complete with mayonnaise." He lifted his
eyebrows hopefully.

She laughed. "Tomato. You make the sandwiches and I'll
handle the coffee."

He led the way into the kitchen and stopped just inside. "If we can find anything after Willamina's organizing."

"Soon you'll find everything is convenient."

She'd bought a one-cup coffee maker and a K-cup carousel filled with mixed brands. "What kind?" She turned the holder. "Dark roast. Columbian. Decaf. Starbucks."

"Kona?" he said teasingly.

She gave him a withering look. "I think you'll need to get a package of that…or go to Hawaii."

"I've never been," he said, cutting a big tomato into slices. "Bread? Bread?"

Megan pointed. "Try the pantry."

He did and returned with a loaf. "Whole wheat."

"Willamina believes in healthy eating. Now, about Hawaii. I've always wanted to go. Annabelle, Lizzie and I talked about it, but life gets in the way."

"Let's just take off and go," he said.

It did sound good. She liked this easy camaraderie and started to jest, "Sure. Call the airlines," but instead she just watched as he applied the mayonnaise and slapped the bread on the sliced tomatoes.

They took the food into the den. She sat on the couch with the lap tray, and he sat in the easy chair. They put their cups on the coffee table.

He looked around. "This will be especially nice in winter with a fire going."

Megan nodded and washed a bite down with coffee. "Right now, the fragrant evening breeze blowing through the window is good."

He agreed. "I think I'm ready for Dr. Beauvais."

"The house looks really great. He should be comfortable here. You can tell him about historic Savannah, and he can tell you about Paris."

His eyebrows lifted. "Symon says he has a villa."

"This isn't exactly a dump."

He cleared his throat. "Certainly not. My decorator has turned it into a historic yet cozy showplace."

"That's better." She set her empty tray on the coffee table.

"It may be a while before you and I have a chance to talk again," he said. "I mean, Dr. Beauvais arrives tomorrow. The wedding's next week. We're finished here. You'll move in with Miss B while work is being done on your house."

She took a sip of coffee, thoughtful, then gazed at him. "We haven't really talked."

"That's what I mean. Thank you for including me in your life like your friends have. Maybe it's time I answered your question."

"You don't have to answer."

"I'd like to. Now, if you care to listen..."

Did she? Accepting Noah as a friend didn't mean they'd relate on a more personal level. Like with Symon. He could talk all day about his personal life, but that would never lead to more than friendship.

After that little lecture to herself, she nodded. From the serious look on his face she knew he would talk about Loretta.

His face turned toward her. "What I felt for Loretta was love as I understood it. But I wasn't ready for a wife. We both had college to get through. We enjoyed the moment instead of thinking about a lifetime. Those were good days. But when I'm concerned about the mention of Loretta, it's not what I lost, but what she lost. How her life turned out so different than she had envisioned and ended at such a young age."

Megan nodded. Talking things over had a way of putting things in perspective, Aunt B said. Megan acknowledged his sharing with a nod and told him about the night Michael was at the dinner when it became known that Symon was not just the caretaker's son but also a famous author.

"Michael had said he wanted us to leave early, to spend some time together other than while we led tours." Remembering, she related the incident. "Michael went on about the caretaker's son having become a famous writer. Then he asked what he had become, mocking his own job as a low-paid tour guide. He said he needed to think about the future."

Looking over at Noah's interested expression she admitted, "I thought he might be thinking of a future with me." This was different. She didn't have that sweep of having been abandoned, but thought she had joined Noah in thinking beyond one's self and to Michael, who needed help. "Now I wonder if it was just conversation. Or a plea for help."

If Michael did need help, he hadn't turned to her. Maybe Noah was the one who could help him. She saw his kind blue eyes, warm, looking as if he longed to know more.

"If I'm not being too personal," Noah said, "did he think you would be receptive to a future with him?"

She felt perfectly at ease and stated a fact in a light, jesting way. "If you're too personal, I won't answer." She drew a deep breath. "Looking back," she said, "I think my feelings changed from personal about us as a couple to caring about Michael's health. It reminded me of having lost my mother to cancer and watching my grandmother's health failing. I couldn't even consider breaking up with him while he was ill."

Seeing that Noah stared at the floor, she had a realization about him. "I couldn't do that," she said softly, "any more than you can abandon him when he needs your help."

"It's tempting," he admitted, "to throw up one's hands, say he's an adult who makes his own decisions and can suffer the consequences." He shook his head. "But is that what we'd want others to do with us, if we were in the wrong or hurting?"

"Of course not," she said. "That's when we need others even more. I'm learning," she said, "that you can associate with a person for quite a while and still not know what's deep inside them."

Noah nodded. "Unless they're willing to share."

She was not thinking about what she had lost but what Michael had lost. "Symon and Paul would have befriended him like they're doing with you," she said. "And Aunt B has a world of wisdom to share."

A wry smile touched Noah's lips. "I agree. But Michael retreats instead of opening up. He pretends all is well until he can't pretend anymore."

They sat in silence for a long moment. Then Megan mused aloud. "If he feels responsible about what happened to Loretta and if he wanted to break up with me, then he might have thought I couldn't handle it."

"If he did, he doesn't know what a strong woman you are."

"Strong?" She scoffed. "How can you say that?"

"If he'd said he wanted to break up, what would you have said?"

"Goodbye," she answered without having to think.

"And," he said carefully, "if he said he wanted to break up because he had things in his life he wasn't handling well?"

She knew that answer, too. "I would have said I'd like to help."

"Exactly," he said softly, his eyes warm and kind and rather sad.

She thought she knew what that meant. What Noah had known all along.

Something was going on that was bigger than holding a grudge because Michael wooed Loretta away from Noah. Bigger than Michael leaving Megan without an explanation.

Bigger than how and in what way Megan and Noah might accept each other.

Another human being needed help, and neither of them could take their relationship any further without considering Michael.

Not that she had any intention of taking anything any further.

Chapter 20

They were all excited about Dr. Beauvais arriving in his private jet. Symon picked him up at the airport and deposited him at the cottage so he could freshen up after the long flight. Dinner was timed for soon after his arrival.

Aunt B always looked as stylish as Megan and Lizzie, some of it attributed to Annabelle's expertise gained through her modeling. But this evening Megan thought Aunt B was exceptionally beautiful and elegant in a simple black silk dress that she complemented well, thanks to her natural attributes and exercise equipment in the basement. Her amethyst jewelry matched the unusual color of her eyes, which was the same as Annabelle's.

Megan, Lizzie and Annabelle watched with her at an upstairs bedroom window for Dr. Beauvais to exit the cottage. Seeing Aunt B finger an earring, Megan thought she wasn't as calm as she looked. "Nervous?"

She exhaled a quivery breath. "Almost as shaky as when he came to take the baby I had to give up."

Their arms went around her. "You look perfect."

She nodded. "I've had years of practice. I can do this. Oh, my."

Their arms dropped as their eyes followed her gaze. A white-haired man in a dark suit was striding up the drive from the cottage. *"Oooh là là,"* Lizzie said. "He's looks like a romantic Frenchman, if I ever saw one."

Annabelle huffed. "When did you ever see one?"

"I read."

"We'd better go down," Megan said.

Aunt B nodded. "Let's hope I don't."

Megan watched her descend the stairs like a true lady in her three-inch black heels. Symon and Noah stood in the living room with Dr. Beauvais. Megan thought him an extremely good-looking man, tall with thick white hair and a handsome face. His dark brown eyes were warm and friendly.

"Miss B," Symon said, "may I present—"

"We've met," she said.

"Mais oui. Bonsoir, madame." He had a rich, deep, kind voice. "And I gave you something."

Her hand moved to her chest, obviously knowing what he meant.

"I brought the matching one." He held a little blue box. "I hope you don't find this insensitive. We could do this in private. Or not at all."

Her face filled with longing. "My friends know all about it." She took the box and lifted the lid. Gingerly moving the tissue to expose a tiny blue bootie, she exhaled audibly as her finger touched the item like a caress. She held the box out for the others to see.

Looking around, she explained. "When they took my baby, one little foot stuck out from the blanket. I reached for it but his wife moved away. I guess she thought I was going to take Toby." She glanced at Dr. Beauvais. "He took the bootie off and gave it to me." Her breath caught. "After kissing Toby's cheek, the bootie was all I ever had of my son."

Aunt B took a shaky breath while the others looked at the bootie. "I have the other one in a chest at the foot of my bed. It represented what I could never have. I also kept things from Symon, the son I adopted emotionally, in that room. The Lord gave me Symon."

Mutual affection showed on their faces and in their eyes. Aunt B closed the box. "Would you put this on the table over there?" she said, and Annabelle did. Aunt B stepped over to Dr. Beauvais and embraced him. "*Merci beaucoup.* Thank you. Nothing could please me more."

Megan suspected she'd forgotten everyone for a moment except Dr. Beauvais. "I brought photos," he said, his eyes as emotional as hers.

"We'll look at them later. First, let's have dinner and get acquainted." She gave a little laugh. "Symon, would you make the introductions, please?"

"Symon has already told me a lot about each of you, *mes amies.*" Dr. Beauvais planted a kiss on the back of Annabelle's, Lizzie's and Megan's hand. He was a charming man and made them smile. Megan dared not look at Noah, lest he think his kiss on her hand had meant any more than this one, which was a friendly gesture.

And of course it hadn't. Her reaction had been different because the situation had been different. This was a pleasant first meeting with an older man expressing a cultural greeting. With Noah, it had marked the beginning of her accepting him on a professional and personal basis.

There! With that settled in her mind, she followed along with the others to the dining room, where Dr. Beauvais and Willamina were introduced. Megan expected her to make some remark when he kissed her hand, but she just glanced at her hand then at him, rolled her eyes and marched back into the kitchen.

Aunt B, having become acquainted with Noah's penchant for prayer, asked him to say the blessing. After the amen, she said, *"Bon appetit."*

They began to fill their plates with the lavish dinner from the sideboard, and Aunt B directed them where to sit. "Annabelle, you and Symon might sit across from Dr. Beauvais since you'll be asking—"

"Henri, *s'il vous plait,*" the handsome smiling man said, the lines fanning out from his dancing eyes and his white hair gleaming from the glow of the chandelier. He rather reminded Megan of how Noah might look in a few decades.

Aunt B nodded and said, "Corabeth." Then the two exchanged words in French and both smiled.

Corabeth? Glancing around, Megan saw the shock resting on everyone's faces, except Noah's, whose eyes questioned. She leaned close and he tilted his head toward her. She explained, "She's Aunt B or Miss B to everybody."

His eyes danced with light, reminding her of Michael's teasing eyes that had appealed to her when she first saw him. But this wasn't Michael and she shouldn't be standing there looking at him, so she focused on the sideboard and walked toward it.

"Does that make me Elizabeth?" Lizzie said, walking up to the French-speaking couple, who had seemed to forget they were in Savannah, Georgia and not Paris.

"Whatever you want," Aunt B said, actually looking like she'd dropped ten years from her age. She was a lovely woman. Megan just didn't think of that often. She was just Aunt B.

"Mercy," Lizzie said. "Let's keep it Lizzie."

Aunt B spoke gently. "I believe that's *merci.*"

Lizzie scrunched her face. "Not in my French class." She began to tell about their escapades and how they had driven their teacher crazy.

"We'd say *merci* as mercy and with a southern accent." She exaggerated her natural accent as she continued with *Je m'appelle* being "my apple" and *s'il vous plait* becoming "silver plate."

Henri seemed delighted with Lizzie. "What about *je vous aime*?"

"I try not to mess up the phrase about love." She exhaled. "But love just doesn't happen to me."

By that time they'd taken their seats. *"Mon amie."* Henri turned his face toward Lizzie, sitting next to him and across from Megan, who was beside Annabelle. "You're young. You have plenty of time."

"Well, I hope so." Lizzie snapped her napkin, then laid it on her lap. "I haven't had my heart flutter since I tackled Georgie in the sixth grade and kissed the tar out of him. I hope those days aren't gone forever."

Symon added to the lighthearted chatter. "I was twenty-nine when Annabelle took over my heart and mind and feelings when I wasn't supposed to even notice her. I mean, when love comes, it's not a matter of maturity anymore. You just have to rein yourself in and remember Miss B is watching."

Annabelle laid her hand on Symon's arm. "I fought it. Lied to myself. But Symon stole my heart against all my warnings. And resolve. Nothing worked."

"This just makes me sick," Lizzie said. "Why can't it happen to me before I get too old?"

"Oh, now, hold on there, *mon amie*," Henri said. "Not that I'm old, but I have been around for several decades. I lost my first wife and thought I'd never love again. But it sneaked up on me. Now I've lost my second wife and believe me, I know how moonlight, and candlelight, and roses, and perfume, and good cooking can be all wrapped up in another person. You just don't get too old for—" he kissed his fingers and held them up in the air "—love."

Megan thought that was supposed to be typical of an Italian rather than a Frenchman, but it sounded romantic anyway. His accent was delightful.

"Then there's hope?" Lizzie said.

"You bet," Henri said.

Megan looked at Aunt B, who wore her tranquil, poised expression, though a smile tugged at the corner of her lips. Just as Aunt B was looking at her plate, Megan didn't feel like looking directly at…anybody, either. So she spoke to Lizzie. "Maybe you and I should move to Paris."

Lizzie grinned as if she knew some kind of secret, and the slant of her green eyes narrowed more than SweetiePie's ever did. "Not yet. You have B and B renovations to plan." Most likely everyone at the table other than Henri and Noah knew she had an underlying meaning.

"Speaking of homes, Henri," Aunt B said. "Symon says you have a lovely villa. I'd love to hear about it."

"It's located in the Loire Valley," he began. His voice was deep and musical. His descriptions expressed his love for his home. He spoke of the beautiful river that gave the valley its name. He painted a word picture of vineyards, wine estates, cathedrals, castles, hot-air balloons and bike trails.

"Oh," Annabelle said accusingly to Symon. "That's why you want to honeymoon there. So you can write about it."

"You guessed it," he said. "Maybe you shouldn't tag along." She swatted his arm with the back of her hand and they exchanged those loving looks again.

"It is a rather fairy-tale existence," Henri said. "In fact, the author of *Sleeping Beauty* found his inspiration there for the story."

He touched on the history, from kings to courtesans, Henry II, Joan of Arc and Leonardo da Vinci who lived near the Loire Valley. "Corabeth," he said then, "I've heard your city has a great history. Perhaps you will share that with me while I'm here."

She discreetly touched her lips with her napkin. "I'd love to," she replied.

Megan met Noah's quick glance. They stared a moment then grinned, and she had to put her napkin over her mouth to keep from laughing. So much for Noah or Megan telling Dr. Beauvais all about Savannah's history.

When Aunt B refused dessert, Henri glanced at her plate,

leaned back and said, "I couldn't eat another bite. This is a fantastic meal. Please tell Willamina—"

"What?" Willamina stood in the doorway. "That Paris don't have nothing over southern cooking?"

He laughed heartily. "Exactly."

"Mercy," she said, and they all laughed.

Henri took a deep breath and became serious when Aunt B said, "We might look at the photos now."

"The briefcase is on the table in the foyer," Symon said.

Aunt B and Henri left the room as Willamina began setting desserts on the sideboard. "Banana pudding," Noah mused when he walked over and picked up a dessert dish. "Now this is like coming home for sure."

"My choice, too," Megan said.

He handed her the dish and picked up another for himself. "Thanks." She glanced over her shoulder then turned back and spoke softly. "This is so amazing. Aunt B gave birth to Toby. Dr. Beauvais raised him until he died at age eleven. So those two are Toby's mom and dad."

"Amazing, too," Noah said, "that she's so open about it." He took a bite of the banana pudding and moaned with delight.

They returned to their places at the table along with the others, and after a bite of the moan-deserving dessert, Megan said, "It could have turned out differently. Aunt B has said she could have chosen to hate her parents instead of forgiving them."

Symon put in, "And if she hadn't disclosed her secret about giving up the baby, she and I wouldn't have the wonderful relationship we do."

"Yes," Annabelle added, "and you wouldn't have gone to Paris to find out about Toby. And Henri wouldn't be here now."

"And too," Symon added, "we might not be planning a honeymoon at a villa in the Loire Valley."

"And Aunt B wouldn't have turned into Corabeth," Lizzie quipped, then sighed heavily. "My life stays the same while all those unexpected things happen to everyone else. All those ifs." She turned her face toward Noah. "Let's not leave you out. If Megan hadn't forgiven you for spying on her, you wouldn't have the cottage job or the B and B job or know Symon and Paul." She grinned and batted her eyelashes. "Or me."

She had to add Megan. "And if Michael hadn't left, you and Noah probably wouldn't be friends."

The accepting smile Megan felt form on her face vanished when she looked across at Noah, who stared at his pudding then glanced around at the others. "Speaking of leaving, that's something I want to talk about. Around the time you return from your honeymoon," he said, looking at Annabelle and Symon, "I plan to leave for the Bahamas, but—" He held up a hand. "I'm getting ahead of myself. I need to tell everyone, including Miss B. and Henri, since he will be staying at my home."

Megan looked down. She knew Lizzie was staring at her. Annabelle and Symon acknowledged his disclosure, then began talking about something else.

Megan felt the sting of abandonment again. Was Noah like Michael, leaving unfinished business?

Maybe it was a family trait.

Just when she thought they'd become friends, had an unspoken understanding. She trusted him. She'd decided Michael's abandonment had not been because of her, but because of his own problems.

She could trust Noah. She'd come to like him. She wanted to be around him. And now he would leave.

Maybe their talking about Hawaii gave him the idea of the Bahamas. Likely he wasn't going alone.

Well, that was not her business. He was not her business. And if she were a vindictive woman, neither would her B and B have anything to do with his business.

She studied her spoon, stirring her pudding.

It seemed to have lost its flavor.

Chapter 21

Nothing else was mentioned about Noah's announcement during the following days. Megan told herself there was no need to bring it up. He had his own life. He could do as he pleased.

Even Lizzie refrained from any insinuations or outright statements. When Megan said, "Maybe you and I should go to Paris after all," Lizzie shook her head and said, "I thought I had discernment. I've got to reexamine my discernment."

Megan scoffed. "I sure don't have any."

They continued packing up and moving in with Aunt B and working their evening jobs. During the mornings there were still wedding plans to finalize.

After a couple days Henri and Aunt B took a private carriage tour and asked for Carl as the driver. Megan figured Noah had set that up. She wondered if Henri would kiss Aunt B's hand. Actually, she'd seen him kiss a lot of hands. Cultural, for him, and charming. Some might say romantic.

Well, she decided it was germy. Not from a Parisian. Only from a Savannahian who was headed for the Bahamas.

Finally, they were all to gather at Aunt B's for lunch. Megan and Lizzie sat in rocking chairs on the wide front porch when Henri, driving Aunt B in her car, rolled up the driveway and around into the garage. Symon and Annabelle were already inside.

When Noah drove up in a van and started on the walkway to the house, Lizzie jumped. "Excuse me," she said. "Necessity calls."

Megan didn't think Lizzie was plagued with incontinence. She felt abandoned. Maybe it was deliberate. And maybe for the best. She had no reason to avoid Noah. As soon as he stepped onto the porch, she asked, "Is Henri settling in all right?"

He leaned against the tall white column next to the banister. "Oh, yes. He walks around the neighborhood, visits the shops and antique stores, talks to everyone he sees. Keeps himself busy, and in the evenings we get along great."

Megan nodded. She could hear the rise of voices. Apparently everyone had gathered in the living room. She stood, and as she started to pass Noah he caught hold of her arm.

"Megan," he said, "I want you, in particular, to go to the Bahamas with me. Please. Consider it."

Her breath caught. She moved to pull away but felt the light pressure of his hand. Her face must look as stunned as she felt.

"I'm going to tell the others, too, but I wanted to ask you in private."

She could not make sense of this. At least she hoped she couldn't. Moving her arm from his grasp she turned and he followed her into the living room.

Aunt B and Henri mentioned having gone to Forsyth Park in which the fountain was modeled after the fountain at Place de la Concorde in Paris. Megan tried to focus on the conversation about carriage rides, renovations, Carl being invited to the wedding, on and on, but she barely heard. Something else occupied her mind.

That something was more questions.

Noah wanted her to go with him to the Bahamas?

She didn't know whether to be glad he thought that much of her. Or insulted that he thought that little of her.

What did he mean? And he said he would talk to the others about it. If he had any sense at all he couldn't tell them…ask them… Of course, he didn't mean anything immoral. Did he? Surely he knew just the two of them couldn't…

Soon the conversation turned to Henri joining the younger men for their morning swim at the fitness center. Henri complimented Noah and his hospitality, saying he felt right at home.

"That brings me to something I want to talk to you about," Noah said, and Megan felt herself stiffen.

"I mentioned to some of you that I'm going to the Bahamas in about three weeks."

"Ooooh, Bahamas," Lizzie said. "Are we invited?"

"In fact, you are."

Megan told her mouth not to drop.

"That's why I wanted to talk to all of you together. My church sponsors annual mission trips. My dad donates supplies and workers. This year we want to help in an area that was devastated by a hurricane and in desperate need of everything."

Megan hoped she wouldn't bawl. She'd misjudged him. At least she was learning that she should not jump to conclusions. His intentions were the best, and he'd given her a special invitation. He wasn't trying to get her alone for some ulterior motive.

Would she go? At that moment she couldn't think of any other place she'd rather be. Not even Paris or Hawaii.

"It's not a vacation," he said. She wasn't thinking of that. Just about a fine, honorable man.

"There's nothing luxurious about it," he warned, "except the setting. This is one of the poorest communities in the northern Bahamas. It's third world in status. A place called Eleuthera. The latest hurricane that threatened us here on the East

Coast did a great deal of damage in the Bahamas. The roof of a church was completely blown away."

He had everyone's attention as he talked about it. "After church on Sunday we'll invite those interested, even if it's only for donations, to stay after the service for more information. Maybe you'd like to join me there. And Henri, even though I won't be home, you're welcome to stay at the house—"

"What? Can't Eleuthera use a doctor?"

"Well, sure."

Henri's handsome face broke into a smile. "Corabeth, I'm sure they could benefit from your teaching experience."

She nodded as if this were an everyday occurrence. "Yes. And if my girls go, they should have a chaperone."

Megan had a feeling Aunt B might be the one who could use a chaperone.

Annabelle and Symon gazed at each other then shrugged. "Sounds like a worthwhile project," Symon said. "I'd like to hear more about it."

Aunt B laughed lightly. "I think we just settled where we'll go to church on Sunday."

Sometimes Megan felt she spent entirely too much time deciding what to wear to church, but not that Sunday. She decided on one of her favorite outfits—a dark brown denim skirt and a knit crepe U-neck tank accompanied by an aqua lapel jacket with quarter-length sleeves.

She added a wide belt, slipped a wood bangle bracelet onto her wrist and chose a metallic leather clutch. Viewing herself in the mirror she thanked God for her many blessings and reprimanded herself for ever allowing negativity to dominate her thinking.

Aunt B had quoted the scripture many times about to whom much is given, much is required. And she lived by that. She was a generous woman. Even if none of them went on the trip with Noah, there were still many ways they could contribute.

She really wanted to go. She wanted to feel like she was helping the truly needy in some tangible way and not just with giving money. She needed to be honest, too. She wanted to go with Noah. Know him better. She had not been fair to him in her attitude. She had been too quick to judge.

Noah's dad met them in the church foyer and had an usher lead them to a pew in the beautiful historic church. Megan loved the architecture of old churches. So much detail had gone into the construction and design. The soft organ music inspired reverence. She wondered why Noah hadn't met them, but when the choir entered their loft she saw Noah with them. Of course, he was a singer. She hoped he didn't notice she stared. On second thought, if he knew, that meant he stared, too.

After the worship service, Noah's dad led the presentation about the mission trip and the area in need. He added that the surrounding villages and cities delighted in having American visitors visit with them in their homes and churches.

Noah reported on his experiences in other places in the Bahamas during a couple of summers several years ago. Other volunteers, most of whom made an annual trip, reported on the work and need.

The pastor's wife approached Aunt B following the meeting and said she knew the church and mission groups would be delighted to have her and Annabelle, known for her testimony and singing, accompany her to various churches.

After church they went to lunch at The Olde Pink House in the heart of the historic district. *"C'est magnifique,"* Henri said, impressed with the eighteenth-century mansion. Megan intrigued him with the story of James Habersham Jr., who supposedly hanged himself in the basement in 1799.

While they enjoyed a meal of traditional southern fare, their conversation turned to the mission project at Eleuthera.

"Paul won't leave the Pirate's Cave that long," Lizzie said. "He will be delighted to donate—" she pointed at herself and added with a smirk "—me."

Megan knew Lizzie would try anything, from nailing on a roof or teaching a class of children. That settled it in Megan's mind. "I'd love to go. I may have to quit my job, but I'm considering that, anyway."

"I came here to visit with Corabeth," Henri said with a warm smile at her. "Whatever she wants to do is fine with me."

Megan thought the blush on Aunt B's cheeks was not a reflection of the mansion's color. "If there's something of value I can do there, I think it would be a great experience."

"If the honeymoon goes well," Symon said, "we might stay in Paris. If not, I'll leave Annie there and—"

He jerked back when Annabelle tried to stab him with her fork. "You keep that up and you'll go on that honeymoon alone."

Noah was pleased. "I'm sure you all know this won't be a vacation, as I've warned you before. Facilities, where there are any, are rustic, even at the mission station. It's a different world. But you might find it interesting to know that Eleuthera is shaped like a mermaid's tail." He laughed at their questioning gazes. "And the narrow island is primarily a beach. Sunsets are spectacular."

The more he talked, the more Megan wanted to be involved in that project. And maybe take time to stroll along the beach and watch the sun set into the horizon.

But first, there was a wedding on the horizon and she almost laughed aloud at the contrast in her mind. Elegant, lovely clothes and makeup. And then make plans for work clothes, sweat and blisters if Noah and the others had reported correctly.

She looked forward to both.

A wedding. Then Eleuthera.

Chapter 22

Noah knew he was a substitute groomsman for Symon's publisher friend who had had a family emergency and couldn't attend the wedding. But he still felt honored.

He also felt that Symon might wear himself out going from window to window, as if peering out would make everything work smoothly. While Paul kept in touch with Lizzie by phone, Noah tried to convince the normally confident Symon that all was well.

"I can't believe it's really happening," he kept saying. "What's taking so long?"

Both Paul and Noah reported every move to him because his pacing and peering didn't register.

While reception tables waited on the back lawn, Miss B's spacious front lawn was a picture-book setting. The pastor, Miss B and Henri exited her antebellum mansion and greeted the guests sitting in the white wedding chairs. They faced the arbor decorated with green vines intertwined with white satin ribbon and yellow roses. The guests had a view of the spacious lawn bordered by live oaks and flowing Spanish moss.

Noah thought Henri had described it best when he'd said earlier, *"Enchanté."*

"Almost time," Noah said when the male violinist and the singer began "The Love of God." With all eyes watching the violinist in this perfect setting, the pastor rose to stand in the arbor. Symon, Paul and Noah made their way from the cottage and through the cars on the driveway and walked across the lawn to take their places at the arbor.

At the appointed time, Megan stood between the great white columns on the porch of the mansion. She descended the steps and moved slowly down the aisle of white carpet.

Noah swallowed hard, could think of no adequate words to describe her, so his mind repeated what Henri had said. *Enchanté.*

She was a lovely classic vision in light green. *Spring green,* he supposed. The form-fitting long silky dress had material over one shoulder, leaving the other one bare. Her hair fell around her shoulders, spread out from her lovely face, and she was smiling as if she was the happiest girl in the world.

He forced his gaze to Lizzie, coming behind Megan and wearing the same style dress in pale yellow. He could only imagine the reason she hadn't yet found Mr. Right was because none were right. She was a wonderful, beautiful woman.

As the two girls reached the arbor to turn and stand on the other side, Megan glanced at him. Maybe she was thinking Michael should be there and not him. She'd said she had begun to see him as separate from Michael. But in that moment, he felt like a substitute again. Not honored, but inappropriate. If Michael hadn't run, he'd be the one who was a groomsman.

Then his awkward moment turned to thoughts of how Megan might feel. She's the one who had been treated unfairly. The one who had every reason to feel self-conscious and uneasy and wonder if she were the object of gossip.

He said a silent prayer, looked over at her and smiled.

She smiled back. Her warm brown eyes seemed to say all was well.

The violinist began to play the wedding march.

Symon breathed, "Oh, my."

Noah feared Symon might keel over as he looked at the vision who appeared to be floating down the runway of white carpet. He'd heard his mom talk about clothes making the woman. Looking at those three beautiful friends, he knew it was the women who made the clothes.

He had that same feeling he'd had when he first saw the three women together at the mall. They'd been gorgeous. Now that was enhanced a hundredfold. The beauty queen, dark hair piled high. Diamonds or rhinestones in her hair and at her ears, then the soft-looking white silky dress covered with lace. It hugged her figure and spread out behind her for a couple feet along the carpet.

They managed to get through the ceremony and Symon seemed to breathe easier after the pastor said, "I pronounce you husband and wife. You may kiss the bride."

Noah experienced that moment of yearning for that something and someone special that could end like this romantic union of two people obviously in love.

His glance at Megan showed her looking at them as if wishing the same, in spite of her having said she didn't want a man in her life.

The photographer had been taping the entire ceremony, so they didn't need to pose for photos. Except one. Mudd and SweetiePie were let out of the house. Mudd wore a black bowtie, and SweetiePie had a yellow flower in her hair. They were such an important part of the bride and groom's love story that they had to be in a photo.

Then there had to be a second photo when the flower fell off and Mudd ate it.

The pastor announced the reception would be at the back of the mansion.

Willamina had directed the catering service, and the back-yard was beautiful with white tables with umbrellas and white chairs dotting the lush green lawn. Long tables were filled with food, with a special one for the wedding cake and the sheet cakes. Bowls of punch were ready for the crystal glasses. There were all sorts of finger foods and silver bins into which one could dip out the food. Quite a wedding feast.

Aunt B made sure Noah and his parents were introduced to everyone. His dad, Henri and Carl seemed to take a special liking to each other.

The wedding party decided they wouldn't change until after Annabelle and Symon did. They'd want to say a last goodbye before Paul would drive them to the airport to board Henri's private jet and fly off to the Loire Valley.

When his parents said goodbye, his mom thanked Megan for helping Noah place his furniture. His dad said he'd looked over the plans for changes in her home and thought they'd be perfect.

As the sun began to make longer shadows along the lawn and the last guests were leaving, Miss B, Henri, Clovis and Carl were sitting at one of the tables. Noah walked over to the one where Megan sat with Lizzie.

"We were just saying," Megan commented, "my match-making plans for Carl may be taking a detour toward Aunt B's best friend."

"Well," Lizzie said, "Annabelle and Symon are perfect examples of the unexpected partnership."

They all agreed it had been a perfect wedding. Carl rose to leave, and after their goodbyes, Miss B suggested the others go inside so the cleanup crew could do its job.

Noah took his cell phone from a side table and put it in his pocket. When they settled in the living room, he felt like he really was a part of this group. That feeling of being a substitute had vanished.

He'd been Symon's groomsman today. He was host to Dr. Beauvais. He was accepted. Megan was a vision of loveliness and seemed at peace with her life.

Henri said he particularly connected with Carl and looked forward to a historic tour he suggested. Clovis, who would spend a couple days with Aunt B, spoke up. "Carl said you could get more out of it if he took us on a private tour and talked while someone else does the driving."

"Us?" Miss B's eyebrows rose and her eyes widened.

Clovis shrugged. "That's what he said. Henri was talking about going with you on the tours, and Carl said he didn't want to be a third wheel, so he asked me to go along."

Henri and Aunt B nodded as if they had a date.

"Carl is right," Megan said. "A private tour is…" She paused. "Um, best."

She shot a quick glance Noah's way, and he was sure she grinned. More and more he had to stop and remind himself of his commitment to his cousin. And that acceptance as a friend didn't mean he could let his thoughts run wild. He needed to try and be content with feeling more accepted by Megan than any time in the past.

His phone vibrated, and he took it from his pocket. His jaw dropped as he stared at the number. He stood.

"Something wrong?" Miss B asked.

Maybe a wrong number. He wanted to say that but knew in all good conscience, he couldn't. He lifted the phone to his ear. "Hello?"

"Noah?"

"Is this—?" He was reluctant to say the name but everyone's eyes were questioning. They likely knew. He knew.

"It's me, Noah. Michael."

Noah mouthed, "Michael."

"How's…" Michael's voice sounded as tentative as Noah felt. "How's Megan?"

Noah looked at the couch where Megan sat next to Lizzie. She stiffened and leaned forward as if she might stand, her eyes questioning. Then she leaned back again, lifting her chin. She must have realized it was his phone, and not hers, that Michael had called. Her bare shoulder rose slightly as if this didn't matter.

Lizzie's gaze at Noah was one of warning, and Noah half expected her to come and tell Michael off or stomp the phone. Megan whispered something to her. Lizzie's shoulders slumped as she emitted a heavy sigh.

He lifted a hand and said, "Sorry."

Miss B nodded and he walked out onto the porch.

"Are you there?" Michael said.

"I'm here. And Megan is fine." He almost laughed at the irony of describing her as fine. He stepped down from the porch and walked out onto the lawn where the remnants of the wedding were almost gone. Workers seemed to be looking for any errant flower petal or damage to a blade of grass.

"She's a remarkable woman." If Michael wanted details, he should call her directly. "She does not deserve this secrecy and confusion."

"What have you told her?"

"Nothing. I've listened to her tell me what she knows of you, and some of it confuses me, too. She thought you were divorced."

"Did you tell her different?"

"I said I would keep your confidences and I will. That's not easy. I feel like I'm hurting Megan, too, knowing things but saying nothing. But she knows Loretta is dead."

Noah waited so long he feared the batteries would go dead. That said a lot about Michael's state of mind. "You know, it would make things easier for me if you told Megan everything. My side of things."

"Easier? Michael, that would be a cop-out. You have to take responsibility. You have to face it."

"I'm trying."

"I know. And I respect you for that."

"Resp—" Michael didn't even finish the word. Could only scoff.

"Give it to the Lord, Michael."

"Yeah. I know you say that. Sorry. Doesn't work with me." The sharpness in his tone turned softer. "You're sure she's okay?"

"Yes, Michael. She's here at Miss B's. Her friends' wedding just ended a short while ago."

"Annabelle and Symon," he said.

"Yep."

"That got to me, too. I can't see me doing that. I know Megan is…well, you know if you've been around her for a while."

"You owe her an explanation of some kind. But I can't counsel you over the phone."

"I'm doing what you suggested, Noah. Working in construction."

"That sounds good, Michael. And I'm glad you called. It's good hearing your voice. By the way, where are you?"

On the way back into the house, Noah knew he should be elated. Michael had called. He was working. Trying. And Noah sort of wished he wasn't thinking about scripture right now and that God had mysterious ways of working things for good. Things might just be working for good…for Michael. And Megan.

He went inside. "That was Michael."

They already knew that. A few glances slid toward Megan, but she sat stiffly, demurely, probably pretending not to be interested. Miss B asked, "How is he?"

"He sounded much better than when I last talked with him. At least I know…" He paused and sat in the nearest chair. "I know where he is."

Lizzie broke the lengthy silence. "Well?" she demanded, "Where is he?"

Noah dreaded giving the response.

"Eleuthera."

Chapter 23

Rain fell for two days. From the sky and not from her eyes. Megan smiled about that. Even though her outside entrance to the upper floor of her house would be delayed before materials would be taken in for renovations, that was fine. Rain wouldn't last forever and she had no deadline for finishing the B and B.

She liked not having to go to work. She'd quit the job and began to sketch more than she had in a while. Mudd's having eaten SweetiePie's yellow rose had been an inspiration. Now that she was staying at Aunt B's, the animals provided a lot more incidents worth drawing. Annabelle had already discussed her ideas for children's books that Megan could illustrate.

During the rain and when the sun appeared again, they continued with plans for the Eleuthera trip. Noah and Henri were at the house often. Noah would come to check on the progress at the cottage and expected completion before Symon and Annabelle returned.

Aunt B didn't ask and Lizzie didn't tease about whether

Megan still intended to go to Eleuthera. Noah talked about how to dress, or underdress, really, and although supplies were sent ahead of them, they should pack plenty of sunblock and work gloves.

Noah reported that the area churches, schools and mission stations near Eleuthera were looking forward to the American visitors to share whatever they would.

Megan thought Noah's eyes often questioned. She hadn't, except for the evening Michael called Noah. After going to bed and staring at the dark ceiling she'd asked herself, *Will I go? Should I go? To see Michael? To be near Noah?*

Those questions weren't exactly a prayer, so she tried again and asked God to lead her. He led her to sleep and when she awakened she knew the answer to all her questions. It was, *Yes*.

She would do what she'd decided in the first place. Share, reach out to others. And while doing so, face the music.

Megan, Lizzie, Aunt B, Henri and Noah flew from Savannah and met up with fifteen people from his church at Ft. Pierce, Florida. They boarded Mission Flight International to Eleuthera. Already, their orientation prepared them for the welcoming they received. Quite soon Megan and Lizzie were paired with other females who would stay in a beachside building. Male workers would bunk in one nearby.

Aunt B and the pastor's wife would stay with the Bahamian pastor and his wife. Henri and another physician would stay with a doctor near the hospital.

Symon and Annabelle flew in the day after the mission group arrived. She would stay with Aunt B, sing and speak at meetings and talk about grooming and nutrition. It delighted everyone to have the former beauty queen include young people and children in her visit.

Each day at Eleuthera began with sitting on blankets or sand for morning devotions on the beach. The devastation of the already-poorest section of the island was vast. Megan knew her personal problems were small compared to these people's, whose homes and businesses had been lashed by violent winds and torrential rains.

The brave spirit of the people was impressive. The mission group came to help, and she experienced the truth of the adage that when you help others, you receive more than you give. Yet, the people appreciated every measurement taken to see what size boards were needed for repair, every board replaced, any damage repaired, ruined furniture removed, all suggestions and advice.

"I like my job in Savannah," Noah said one morning while near Megan in a house they were helping repair. "But there's just something more fulfilling about donating my time to needy people."

"Okay," she quipped, "you can stop the work on my house."

"No, no," he said quickly and grinned. "Present company excluded."

She smiled. "I know what you mean. It's easy to get wrapped up in one's self. This puts things in perspective."

Megan believed she had things in perspective until about midweek, when the temperature rose and the winds picked up. Some of the workers would be needed to keep those repairing the church roof supplied with water. Noah had already told her Michael was working on the roof.

She saw Michael and Noah working near Symon on the steep roof. Both looked her way when the women neared the church. Their hair shone golden and pink in the morning sun. Both wore jeans and T-shirts and looked the part of strong, muscular builders. Noah might be a bit trimmer, maybe thanks to his swimming.

She lifted her hand. So did Michael, and his water bottle rolled off the roof.

Lizzie said, "Noah didn't wave. He must have thought you were waving at Michael."

Megan accepted that, appreciating Lizzie's discernment

and indirect way of making a statement. Lizzie knew her well enough to know the wave was like *aloha* in Hawaii or *bonsoir* in France. They could mean both hello and goodbye.

Someone on the ground yelled, "Here you go," and threw a plastic bottle of water up to Michael, who caught it. Workers were draining bottles and throwing them down, and volunteers would toss full ones up to the roof.

Megan and Lizzie, with most of their attempts, were more humorous than helpful. They decided they'd hand the bottles to guys more adept at reaching the workers high on the steep roof. She hoped the wave let Michael know she wasn't suffering, she wasn't angry and she wasn't there to question him.

On the day the roof was finished, they planned a dedication service for Sunday morning. On Saturday evening, however, they had their usual evening service on the beach. Several from the city would attend. They set up a tarp and a few beach chairs for those not wanting to sit on the ground.

Now that the roof was finished, she supposed Michael would move on with the work crew to another project. When Noah strolled up with some of the volunteers, he approached her. "Michael said he might talk to us later today."

"Us?" she questioned. But this was not the time for that. Her friends were getting out of cars and heading toward them across the sand. Megan realized how good it was to see Annabelle, Aunt B and even Henri after their being separated for a few days

The pastor leading the service had asked some of them to say a few words. Henri mentioned the great cathedrals and sculptures in Paris. Megan told of the historic churches and of many periods in Savannah. That led right into the pastor's remarks, who said they had a church ready for use right now. But they were having church right there on the beach. He reminded them the church is in the heart of man, wherever that might be. They all joined in singing "This Is My Father's

World." Megan smiled hearing the gifted voices of Annabelle and Noah.

The beautiful Annabelle ended the service by singing "The Love of God." Her and Symon's glances silently spoke loudly of human love, too.

Megan reflected on that. The human love of personal relationships and the human love of helping others, being there for them in a time of need. Like the mission group was for the people here. Like Noah was for Michael. Often, she had to remind her selfish heart that she respected Noah for that.

After the service, as others were going in for a prayer of thanks and dedication of the church, Megan saw a familiar figure strolling down the beach. Michael must have known the service was taking place and waited for it to end. Noah noticed, too, and stepped near her.

"Us?" she said, taking up the conversation where it ended before the service.

"That's what he said." He looked apologetic. "I should leave and let you two—"

"Leave?" She questioned. "Since we met, you've tried to help me understand Michael. You've prayed about him and have wanted to help him, and have kept his secrets. Now, when it comes down to the grand finale, you want to leave?"

"It's not what I want."

"What do you want, Noah?"

"I want you…to…" Whatever it was pained him. "Deep inside, I want what's best for you."

He sat in the chair next to her as Michael stepped under the tarp.

"Megan," he said, "all the apologies and excuses in the world won't change anything. I was a coward to leave like I did. I am not the man I pretended to be."

Megan wanted to help. He looked so uncomfortable, she thought he might turn and run. "I read the newspaper article about Loretta."

Michael grasped the pole holding up the tarp. "It's not… just that."

Megan looked over at Noah, who sat stiffly, staring straight ahead, his face taut. "She was—"

"Just say it," Noah demanded.

"Pregnant."

Megan almost couldn't make out the word he said in such a choked voice.

"Sit down, will you, Michael?" Noah said compassionately.

Michael did. He leaned forward and rubbed his face for a while and then straightened. "That's the first time I've been able to say it except that once to you," he said to Noah. He took a deep breath. "She was pregnant."

With eyes closed and his hands rubbing his denim-clad legs, he ground out the words. "She told me at the party. Said we could get married. She was happy. I was shocked. Couldn't imagine her messing up our lives like that. Blamed her. Even accused her of doing that deliberately."

Megan glanced at Noah. Yes, she could tell he already knew. Pain was on his face. This was so horrible, but Michael needed to say it, admit it.

After several gulps he continued. "I killed her with my words before she ran out from the party. Somebody said not to let her leave like that. I don't know if that's why I ran out to find her. I don't know if I cared more about her feelings than I did my own. Regardless, it was too late. So you see…"

Megan saw.

She hated to hear it. But she knew he needed to say it.

"I ruined her life long before she ran into the tree. And I don't know if it was deliberate or an accident. But the result was the same. And I killed…my own child."

How long they sat in silence she didn't know. It felt like an eternity.

"Let me get some water," Noah said. He went over to a box and returned with a bottle.

Michael opened it and drank. That seemed to help and he continued. "I really thought when I returned to college and met Megan my life was turned around." He looked at Megan, and his wry smile made dimples in his damp cheeks. "And it worked." He took a deep breath. "For a while." He shook his head. "You don't want to hear all this."

"Yes, yes we do," Megan and Noah both said.

He breathed deeply. "I really did have the flu during Christmas. That's the time when you do something special for someone special. What could I do? Confess? Keep it all a secret? Pretend for the rest of my life I was not a…not a…"

"A sinner?" Noah said.

"Yeah. Call me what I am."

"It's what we all are, Michael. That's why we need to accept Jesus in our lives. It's possible that Loretta and I could have done wrong. We weren't ready to settle down in marriage."

Michael scoffed. "Not you."

"Yes, me. And believe me, I've thought about knocking your teeth down your throat for what you did to Loretta. And were doing to Megan."

"She looks like she's doing all right."

"She didn't deserve your silent treatment."

"She didn't deserve what I had to offer—a broken life. I was looking for somebody to fix me." He held up his hand. "Don't say it. I know. No person can fix me."

"That's right." Noah went over to where a pair of gloves lay. He picked one up and brought it over. "Michael, what can this glove do by itself?"

Looking at the way Noah held it limply he shrugged. "Nothing."

Noah put his hand into it. "But with this hand in it, it can nail on a roof. It can do nothing alone. It has to have the power behind it."

Michael was nodding. "I get it."

Noah said it anyway. "There's not much we can do on our own. We need God's power in us."

"God forgives, you know," Megan said.

"I don't have a problem with that," Michael said. "I can't forgive myself. Don't know if I ever can. I thought I had, but I went right back into depression. I'm guilty and I know that with time and effort, I can live with it. But not yet."

"I think you just took a giant step," Noah said.

Michael nodded. "I know."

He actually smiled. A sad one. But a smile.

He pulled his chair up in front of Megan and sat down. He took her hands in his. "I'm sorry," he said. "I wasn't honest with you. But I began to be honest with myself. I know I'm not the man for you. But I loved you in my way."

She smiled then. She'd loved him, in a way, too. Liked him, cared about him.

After a gentle squeeze of her hands, he moved away and straightened. "I wasn't ready to open up to Miss B and your friends. Finding out she gave up her baby made me feel worse. I couldn't confess what I did—" his voice choked "—to mine."

She nodded. "I don't know about that kind of guilt, Michael. But Aunt B has helped me realize that there are some things we may never get over. We learn to live with them and get on with our lives. I think you'll be all right."

He looked into her eyes. "Are you?"

"Yes."

"Not angry? Or hurt? Or want me to beg, or anything?"

They both were grinning. Some of that playfulness was in his manner despite the words. "I hoped for that," she said.

"What? Hoped?"

Before she could form a coherent question, he stood and stepped back, holding on to the long pole. "Noah and I always had the same taste in girls. I tried and succeeded in taking Loretta away from him. I knew if you two—"

"Stop it, Michael," Noah demanded. "This is no game." He

glanced at Megan and mumbled, "He reminds me of Lizzie right now."

Megan got a glimpse of how they must have played their games in the past. Except for the one that got out of hand, they probably had fun, had a great relationship. "At least I brought you two together."

Noah huffed. "Michael, I don't know whether to hit you or hug you. I've been trying to get you two together and now you're telling me you were trying to get us together. Will you ever tell the truth?"

"Did it work?"

"We're not...together."

Michael looked from one to the other, scowled and nodded, saying slowly, "Oh."

Megan and Noah glanced at each other, then at Michael, and they all laughed.

Chapter 24

Michael said he'd go to Haiti next with the work crew. More damage had been done there than in Eleuthera. After he left, Noah asked Megan if she'd like to walk along the beach with him. She said yes.

He felt good about Michael. "You know," he said, "I've tried to do what I thought best to help Michael. I've prayed, talked, assured him I was there for him and tried to help you understand him."

"I know," she said, giving him a sidelong glance. "How does it feel to no longer be working on the project of getting us together?"

"Well," he said slowly. "It's only been about forty-five seconds since I was taken out of that responsibility. This is, um, a little new to me." He still wasn't sure. He knew what he wanted, but… "You seemed comfortable with him."

"Yes, but it was getting a little crowded with the three of us all the time."

Did she mean Michael had been in the way? Or Noah?

They kept walking and she said, "I like Michael. But there's nothing personal anymore. He's…history." She smiled at Noah. "I think Haiti will be good for him. I want the best for him. Like you said you wanted the best for me." She paused, then said tentatively, "I don't want you to go to Haiti."

"You don't?" He thought she was teasing him. He warned himself not to be hasty. That wasn't a creek out there. Just the churning dark blue Atlantic Ocean to the east and the calm aqua-green waters of the Great Bahama Bank to the west. He doubted she'd find it romantic to plunge into either.

He stopped and reached down. Then he raised up and held out his hand. "Would you like a shell?"

She nodded. "I'd love one."

She looked at it, held it to her ear, then put it in her pocket. They kept walking. She said, "If we don't turn back we're going to run out of pink sand and walk right off the mermaid's tail."

He stopped, considering what to do. Pretend to be a calm sea or chance being a churning ocean.

"What's on your mind?" she asked.

"I was thinking about Symon and Annabelle's creek."

She looked out the water and back at him. "It looks nothing like the creek."

He began to grin. She looked a little surprised, then he was sure that was an invitation in her eyes.

"You think that creek incident could really compare with walking on pink sand and standing on a mermaid's tail?"

"I don't know," she said and added softly, "yet."

Strange, this sense of freedom. He no longer had to be torn by what he wanted and what he thought might be God's will for her and Michael's lives. He was free to…

Love or lose.

But free to try.

"Megan," he said and reached for her.

She looked at him for a long moment. Her soft glance went

to his hair and so did her hand. "Your hair is gold and orange-pink, like the sky." He felt her fingers brush it aside like a caress, and then she was in his arms.

She didn't pull away. His lips were on hers, tasting the sweet honey of them, and he was holding her close and she was returning his kiss. Vaguely, he remembered something about two kisses, but this was not a game of competing with anyone.

It was a matter of the heart, so he took her by the shoulders and moved her away enough to look into her beautiful face.

Her laugh was happy and sweet. "I've waited a long time for that. We've been walking and walking, and I've been waiting for at least fifteen minutes."

Noah laughed lightly. They hadn't walked for more than five minutes. But the waiting? Yes, he, too, had been waiting a long, long time and hadn't even known it. Something about this seemed right, complete.

He held her head against his chest and hoped the sound of his heart sent the message that he could not speak in words.

Finally, he found a few words. "I've been so afraid of my feelings for you, Megan. I knew right away I could fall in love with you. But it seemed my purpose was to bring you and Michael together."

She was looking up at him, her face aglow, reflecting the colors of the sky. He never wanted to let her go. This was too wonderful to believe. "I will be praying it's God's will you can love me."

Her nose crinkled. "It's fine to ask God, but you might try asking me, too."

"Hmmm," he mused. "I'll think about that." He was glad for the more playful mood. He kissed her lightly and she returned it.

"I want some pink sand," she said.

"What will we put it in?"

There was only one thing he could do. They held hands on the way back to the others. Lizzie must have been watching for them. She looked at the shoe he held and the way he limped along with only a sock on one foot.

She shook her head. "I knew it," she said. Then she made a clicking sound.

Neither Megan nor Noah tried to keep their feelings for each other a secret. But there was little time for anything but Noah's tending to work because he'd been occupied with other things so much during the past weeks.

Henri regretted having to leave but feared he'd wear out his welcome. He wanted Aunt B and any of them who could to visit him at his villa. He had plenty of friends in France, but he'd like to spend time with his new friends. They would make plans for visiting and he might even decide to buy one of those historic homes in Savannah and spend more time there.

Noah called Megan. "I want to date you and for us to get to know each other." He asked her out for Friday evening. She was sitting in a rocking chair on Aunt B's porch when he came to pick her up. "I have something special in mind," he said.

When he drove to The Olde Pink House she thought he probably chose that as a reminder of the pink sand of Eleuthera and their first kiss. He pulled around to the back, and she didn't think much of the pumpkin-shaped carriage and white horse because she'd seen them many times.

Noah led her to it. Carl appeared, dressed in a white suit, and jumped up into the driver's seat. Noah opened the wrought iron door and held out his hand for her to enter. He got in beside her and off they went.

She felt like Cinderella going to a ball with a handsome prince. The clip-clop along the cobbled streets and the sway of the carriage were like music. Carl drove them to a white gazebo at one edge of Forsyth Park with a sign marked "Private."

Noah led her into the gazebo. She knew about this kind of event but had never thought she'd be part of one. She'd heard about the roses and champagne, as the drink of choice, and the chocolate. He handed her the rose and sang a love song to her.

"I wanted to do something special when telling you that I love you. I know it's too soon to ask for a commitment and…"

She didn't let him finish. There was no need. The lips had a language of their own. After a while they walked around on the brick walkways, held hands at the beautiful fountain, spoke softly beneath the moss-laden majestic trees. The sun turned the world into dappled jewels of gold and pink and orange.

The most beautiful of all was the feeling of having found the one you want to spend your life with.

"This is wonderful," Megan said. "How did you ever think of it?"

He smiled down at her, no reserve in his eyes now, no caution, no restraint, just letting her know he loved her. "You began to see me when we took that carriage ride. The words in one of the brochures is BEST HISTORY REPEATS ITSELF. I thought you and I might repeat the carriage ride and begin making our own history."

She nodded. Yes, she was thinking of the adage that those who do not learn from history are doomed to repeat it.

She was already ready for his arms as he said, "I want the history of you and me to be repeated every moment of our lives. Not doomed. But blessed."

"Now, there's a lesson in love," she said. And they put action to the words as they stood in the shadow of a live oak with Spanish moss swaying gently over their heads and a soft breeze singing its love song.

* * * * *

HEARTSONG
PRESENTS

Look out for 4 new
Heartsong Presents books next month!

**Every month 4 inspiring faith-filled
romances will be available in stores.**

These contemporary and historical Christian
romances emphasize God's role in every
relationship and reinforce the importance of
faith, hope and love.

REQUEST YOUR FREE BOOKS!

2 FREE CHRISTIAN NOVELS
PLUS 2
FREE
MYSTERY GIFTS

♡

H E A R T S O N G

P R E S E N T S

YES! Please send me 2 Free Heartsong Presents novels and my 2 FREE mystery gifts (gifts are worth about $10). After receiving them, if I don't wish to receive any more books I can return the shipping statement marked "cancel." If I don't cancel, I will receive 4 brand-new novels every month and be billed just $4.24 per book in the U.S. and $5.24 per book in Canada. That's a savings of at least 20% off the cover price. It's quite a bargain! Shipping and handling is just 50¢ per book in the U.S. and 75¢ per book in Canada.* I understand that accepting the 2 free books and gifts places me under no obligation to buy anything. I can always return a shipment and cancel at any time. Even if I never buy another book, the two free books and gifts are mine to keep forever.

159/359 HDN FVYK

Name	(PLEASE PRINT)	
Address		Apt. #
City	State	Zip

Signature (if under 18, a parent or guardian must sign)

Mail to the **Harlequin®** Reader Service:
IN U.S.A.: P.O. Box 1867, Buffalo, NY 14240-1867

* Terms and prices subject to change without notice. Prices do not include applicable taxes. Sales tax applicable in N.Y. This offer is limited to one order per household. Not valid for current subscribers to Heartsong Presents books. All orders subject to credit approval. Credit or debit balances in a customer's account(s) may be offset by any other outstanding balance owed by or to the customer. Please allow 4 to 6 weeks for delivery. Offer available while quantities last. Offer valid only in the U.S.

Your Privacy—The Harlequin® Reader Service is committed to protecting your privacy. Our Privacy Policy is available online at www.ReaderService.com or upon request from the Harlequin Reader Service.
We make a portion of our mailing list available to reputable third parties that offer products we believe may interest you. If you prefer that we not exchange your name with third parties, or if you wish to clarify or modify your communication preferences, please visit us at www.ReaderService.com/consumerschoice or write to us at Harlequin Reader Service Preference Service, P.O. Box 9062, Buffalo, NY 14269. Include your complete name and address.

HSPDIR13R

LARGER-PRINT BOOKS!

GET 2 FREE
LARGER-PRINT NOVELS
PLUS 2 FREE
MYSTERY GIFTS

Love Inspired®

Larger-print novels are now available...

LILPDIR13R